TUNNEL VISION

TUNNEL VISION

(THRU THE EYES OF A TRANSIT COP)

W. K. Brown

Brownwk.com

iUniverse, Inc.
New York Lincoln Shanghai

TUNNEL VISION
(THRU THE EYES OF A TRANSIT COP)

iUniverse books may be ordered through booksellers or by contacting:

iUniverse
2021 Pine Lake Road, Suite 100
Lincoln, NE 68512
www.iuniverse.com
1-800-Authors (1-800-288-4677)

W. K. Brown Enterprises
P.O. Box 390656
Deltona, Fl 32739
Brownwk.com

ISBN-13: 978-0-595-35050-6 (pbk)
ISBN-13: 978-0-595-79756-1 (ebk)
ISBN-10: 0-595-35050-X (pbk)
ISBN-10: 0-595-79756-3 (ebk)

Printed in the United States of America

Contents

▼

ACKNOWLEDGMENTS

I would like to thank the men and women of the New York City Police Department for their dedication and courage in the service they provide to the people of New York.

Further thanks goes out to my daughter Samantha Brown for all the help that she has given me as the editor of this book. To her I cannot give enough thanks.

Most of all I would like to thank my wife, "Shirley" for she has been my foundation and strength for many years. Without her at my side I do not know if I could have made it through the many years that I gave to the City of New York. I thank her for understanding the times that I could not be with her and our children because of my commitment to the department. For all the strength that she gave me to do a job that she knew I loved, but not more than I loved her and the children. I just wanted to provide for them and to protect them. Without her at my side, none of this would have been possible. Thank you, I will always love you.

Brownwk.com

INTRODUCTION

Hello, welcome aboard, sit down and get comfortable, for you are about to be taken on the ride of your life. In the subway no one knows your name, so few will be used and those used have been changed. Why, because this is the subway and in the subway no one knows your name.

The people you are about to meet could be one of the many that you see or don't see everyday. They will be described by age, gender or race only. They are just faces in the crowd. Faces that mean little or nothing to you. They don't know you and you don't want to know them. As long as no one bothers your peace you could care less about them.

In the subway there are only a few things that matter. Is the train on time, reaching your destination safely and not getting a smelly car. This is the subway and these are the important topics to worry about, no one and nothing else matters.

Welcome aboard, thank you for riding the New York City Transit System, "Watch the closing doors."

A dramatization of fictionalized events.

CHAPTER 1

▼

THE FEW, THE PROUD...

August 1980, a hot summer's morning nine o'clock on a Saturday, eyes' foggy, head the same, waiting to take the NYPD entrance exam. A pencil is placed in front of me along with the answer sheet, my mind is starting to clear, yes I am awake this is not a dream. The proctor hands out the exam and says to start. It's too late to back out now. And so the journey begins.

The test is over before I know. As I leave the answer sheet on the proctor's desk I think to myself, that was too easy, you must have really messed up. As I walk to my car I laugh to myself thinking why did you even show up? You don't want to be a cop. You'll get killed. But this thought passes by quickly. As I think back on the test and how easy it was or I thought it was, the feeling that I didn't pass anyway sort of made me feel better, I thought.

September 1980, a letter comes from the City of New York Personnel. I know what it's about, it's the, "You failed, good try, kiss off" letter. As I open this letter of rejection I cursed to myself, feeling that I could have passed that test, why didn't I. I had the book to study, but thought it was stupid. Those questions they asked, a fifth grader could answer.

As I read this vile paper it suddenly hits me that I have passed. Not only passed but also passed with a 98 percent. This cannot be right. But here it is in black and white. I'm almost a cop.

Two weeks later eight o'clock on a Sunday night the phone rings. It's Police Officer Holden from the New York City Transit Police. He wants to know if I am interested in a position with the Transit Police Department. I questioned him as to what is the Transit Police and what do they do? Also, how did he get my name, since I never heard of the New York City Transit Police Department.

The answer that he shot back was that he had received my name from the New York City Police Department as a possible recruit. Adding that the City police would not be hiring for the next fiscal year. And as a result of that they passed my name onto the Transit Police. "Ok." I said, "But what is the Transit Police? What do you guys do?"

His reply was straightforward, "We cover the subways and buses of the city, but mostly we cover the subways. The pay is the same. The benefits are the same as the city. It's just that we work in the subway. "A Subway cop. I didn't know they existed. Do you guys carry guns?" I asked.

The phone seemed silent for a second. Then came the answer of, "Yes we do. We are real cops. Like I said it's just that we work in the subway. Do you want the job or not?" "Yes," I replied. "Good then be at the academy on East 20th Street in Manhattan at nine o'clock tomorrow morning. Bring your driver's license and birth certificate. Ok see you tomorrow."

December 1980. Well I'm in the academy. I don't believe this. I'm going to be a New York City Transit cop. This is great. The Transit Police had hired one hundred guys and the Housing Police had hired another hundred. Man we got lucky, the city didn't hire anyone or so we were told. All the recruits I talked to liked the idea of being a Transit cop, although we didn't know anything about Transit cops.

January 1981, the Police Department City of New York hires one thousand cops. What's going on here? I thought the regular police wasn't going to hire any-one. What's up with this? The academy is a buzz with the news that the real police just hired a bunch of guys. They are going to be real New York City cops. Working out of precincts, driving blue and white police cars. Not Transit cops in the subway sweating or driving black and white zebra cars, that no one recognizes as a cop car. What happened here? Why?

The answer was not long in coming, long enough but not long. Just long enough for us Transit guys to graduate from the New York City Police Academy. The first class of Transit cops to ever do so. It seems that up until us the Transit police had their own academy, apart from the real police. We were the test class of one type of police training for all cops in the city. So we had to attend the real police academy, you know the big step up.

No wonder most of the time we were treated as second-class citizens or maybe a stepchild. No, that's not true. A stepchild would be treated better than the way Transit recruits were treated by the City Police guys, which ran the academy. At lease we got treated well enough by our instructors when no City guys were around, because they are Transit cops also, teaching in a foreign place.

Oh yeah, the answer as to how come the City did not pick us to be real cops came in like a blow to the head with a nightstick. It seems like anyone who took the entrance exam and scored between 90 and 100 percent went to Transit. Anyone scoring 80 to 90 percent went to Housing, and the rest went to the real police. This meant that if you scored between 70 to 80 percent you got the real job, that's not right. I thought you had to be some kind of smart to be a cop.

The way it was explained was that Transit cops work alone 98 percent of the time, so they must know what they are doing and how to do it. The radios are bad and help could be a long time in coming. Transit cops had to be smart and able to think fast. Housing, well they also work alone sometimes, but not as much as Transit. Their area is smaller and they carry real police radios, so that the big guys can get to them quickly if needed.

The real police, well there are so many of them. Most of the time they work with partners, or are placed only one or two blocks away from each other. Of course they have the best radios that police department money can buy. With a supervisor not far away they didn't have to score too high, they would be guided as to what to do and how to do it.

Transit, not so lucky. As we were told whatever comes up handle it and don't bother the supervisor with petty stuff. If you make a collar, police talk for arrest, you better know why you collared that person and be able to explain it.

Another feel good speech to the Transit guys was that we are the marines of New York City policing. The precinct cops were the army. We were the elite. Thus the battle cry every morning on the roof of the academy. "ACADEMY FALL IN! ACADEMY ATTENTION! ACADEMY, WHO ARE YOU? The response from the Transit recruits rang through the air of Manhattan, "WE ARE THE TRANSIT POLICE SIR, THE FEW, THE PROUD, THE BEST," man what a feeling, yeah right.

For six months three times a day those words shot out over the city. Transit recruits howling to the world that we are someone. That we do exist, even though our instructors would not be associated with us until we had proven that we had the right stuff.

That day came in May 1981 when the recruits were called to muster. The growl from the instructor, "ACADEMY FALL IN! ACADEMY ATTENTION! ACADEMY, WHO ARE WE?" We I thought, he said we.

The recruits seemed stunned. Taken back by the change in the cadence. Proudly and with force we shot back, "WE ARE THE TRANSIT POLICE SIR, THE FEW, THE PROUD, THE BEST." We were on our way, to what we didn't know, but we were on our way.

CHAPTER 2

▼

CHERRY POPPED

We graduated at 0900 from One Police Plaza. Everyone looked great in his or her new uniform, bright, shinny, and ready to go. Later that night I arrived at my new command at ten o'clock, 2200 hours to us now, nervous, not scared, looking to learn the ropes.

First up to greet me is the desk officer who is not very interested in meeting new cops. He looks up from the blotter and snares, "Get a locker and be ready by 2325."

Dressed ready to go, looking for someone to tell me what to do next, no luck. Then, in comes my training officer for the night. "Hi Rookie, I hope you're ready? Come here. I walk over to a wall that has long sheets of papers hanging down from it. The training officer looks me over and smirks "What's your name?" "Kenny," I reply. "Ok, Kenny they call me "Q." "Ok Q, what are all those papers for?"

"Well rookie look on there and find your name. That's the post you got. Then follow down to the next officer's name. You got all the stations in-between. Next to your name is a time, that's when you eat. You get one hour, unless you get a call. Then you get what you got. Be back here at eight o'clock in the morning that's when you go home. Keep your eyes open cause you're going to see some strange things and stuff you won't believe. Anyway just have your ass back here by eight o'clock."

"Was that it?" I thought, "Was that all of the training he was going to give me?" With a final "Be safe kid," my so-called training officer's job was completed. This was it everything else I had to learn on my own. Thank God I was a quick learner. I guess that's why I was picked for Transit.

Over the years the department changed the way new officers were trained. But for me the training was over, I was on my own.

Roll call over, out the door. Then down the stairs to the northbound platform. There's only northbound and southbound in the subway, no east or west. North is heading towards Manhattan. South is heading away from Manhattan, that's it. Get on train. Get off next stop. This station and the next three are mine. All mine. I run the show, if I knew how.

The smell of urine is strong. The lights are low, dull, dim, and not even enough to cast a shadow. Walk over to token booth say hi to clerk. He could care less. Go up the stairs to the street and look around. Damn did someone drop a bomb while I was in the hole? That's what we call the subway.

Most of the buildings are run down, streets dark and dirty, no one in sight. Back down the stairs. Walk the platform, nothing. There is nothing but rats and dirt from one end to the other. Alright now what? I know. Let me get a summons, my first one. Take off hat. Stand halfway up the stairs leading to the booth area, so that I can see the turnstiles. Thirty minutes, forty minutes, one hour, nothing. No one is doing anything. Get on train get off next station, same as the first. Hell, let's try again. Hat off. On stairs looking, looking and trying to get my first summons.

Thirty minutes, forty minutes. Wait. Here comes someone, a lady. She looks around and walks through the slam gate without paying. I got her. A train is leaving the station so now she gotta wait for another one. Now I can take my time in going over to her. Since I got time lets see if she will do something else. I'm looking out at her but she can't see me. I got a good hiding spot. No one but her on the platform, so watching her is easy.

What's she up to? She keeps looking around. She walks down past the garbage can. What's she doing messing around with her skirt and bending down? Her head is moving from side to side keeping a lookout. What is she doing? Oh snap, I know what she is doing. She pulls down her skirt then goes over and sits on the bench.

Here I come. How should I approach? Shit, just do it and let the words come out as they will. "Excuse me Miss, you didn't pay your fare is there a reason? Could I have some ID please?" Very professional I thought as I looked at this well dressed woman. Then came the response, "What the fuck you mean I didn't pay? I always pay my fare. Get the fuck away from me New Jack."

Oh shit, now what? I know she didn't pay, but she is saying she did. I know what I saw. Through my thoughts I hear, "Well what the fuck you still standing here for, get your ass away from me." Wait a minute, who's the cop here? Me. She cannot talk to me that way. What to say? What to say?

"Ma'am, you didn't pay your fare. You are going to get a ticket. Also I saw you urinate on the other side of that garbage can over there, so don't tell me I didn't see you. Come over here with me and I'll show you where you urinated. "You didn't see me piss nowhere," she stated. "Well let's go see," I said.

Well to my surprise she was about right. For there in front of us on the other side of the garbage can was a long brown stain slipping down the wall to the ground, and oh the smell. On the ground beneath this brown mess was a wet spot. I snapped out, "No, you didn't just piss you shit also. What you got to say now?" "Eat it," She said. "Alright give me some ID," I spat back. But do I really want to touch her ID, no paper, no wiping of the butt. Her hands must be filthy. Where are my gloves? I write the three tickets and give them to her.

She says, "Why I'm getting three?" I reply, "One for not paying your fare, one for defecating, and one for urinating." She fires back, "Alright I didn't pay. I did shit but I didn't piss, so I should only get two." I respond by saying, "Miss like I said you didn't pay that's one. I have never heard of anyone taking a shit without pissing also, that's two and three."

Her final thought to me, "Fuck you, you're right but not three. Give me two, the shit and piss should count as one." "Have a good night Miss."

Lord help me. Don't tell me this is how the next twenty years is going to be. When "Q" said, "You are going to see things," I guess he was right. This was my first tunnel vision, there were many more to come.

Tunnel vision, the things you see in the subway. Experiences that cannot be seen anywhere else. Things that people do when they assume that no one is around. The stuff that you just cannot make up. True life. This is life in the unseen world of the subway. The topics of conversations that people would just not believe.

My first visions that I saw came in the Bronx in the early 1980's. The Bronx, a place that seemed to have been forgotten by time, an area of the great City of New York that had come to disarray. The buildings looked like they were in the middle of a war zone. There were areas that you could only walk through with a gun, and then very fast, with your eyes wide open. But yet people still lived here, good people mostly. People that were trying their best to survive this jungle, to make a better life for themselves. Then there were the others, the people that didn't care or had just given up. Lets focus on them, for they made the subway life in the Boogie Down Bronx a ride that could not be forgotten.

Back to my stairway, I got my cherry popped now, so lets see what else the night will bring. Somehow I missed a man that had entered the station. He stands on the northbound platform, head moving from left to right. Now I know this look, he's up to something. A cigarette comes out. He lights it and cups it in his right hand.

I got him. No smoking on the subway. Up the stairs I go. As I hit the platform with the feeling that this is easy pickings. An express train roars pass the station taking any smell of smoke away in its wake. The man sees me and makes a quick move to his right pants pocket. Now I smell no smoke, I see no cigarette, but I know he was smoking.

The approach is good, stance strong, voice well trained, "Excuse me sir there is no smoking on the subway, could I have some ID please." The response, "Who the fuck you talking to? I'm not doing anything, leave me the fuck alone." "Sir I saw you smoking, so please give me your ID." The set of his jaw grew tight and the words that came next were just as tight. "I told you I wasn't smoking. If I was then where is the butt, can you smell any smoke, why the hell are you fucking with me?"

Now I know what I saw, but this guy is putting doubt in my mind. Maybe I didn't see what I thought I saw. Step back get your thoughts together. Take a second to think, this guy is very upset that I accused him and maybe I'm wrong. I stop, I think. Wow, how could I be so wrong? I hear, "What the fuck you still looking at?" The man is rubbing his right pants pocket with his right hand, rubbing harder and harder with each stroke. His face is getting flush. The smell of something burning is starting to hit my nose.

I think, "Oh shit, don't tell me he did that. Don't tell me he put it in his pocket still lit." So I wait. He starts to walk away from me, still rubbing his pocket. I follow. He gets angry and yells out, "Stop following me. What are you a faggot?!" I paid no attention to him and kept focused on his pocket. The smell of burning cloth is getting stronger now. His foot is tapping on the platform. His eye's starting to bulge. Then in a flash he shoves his hand into his pocket and pulls out the cigarette. It's still lit, he throws it onto the track area. Spitting on his hand he rubs his right leg, while letting out a sigh of relief.

With this I again say, "Sir, like I said there is no smoking in the subway, could I have some ID?" In the midst of all kinds of curses he gives me his ID. I wrote the ticket, gave it to him, and asked, "Was it worth burning your leg to avoid a five dollar ticket." The answer, "Go fuck yourself and die."

As I walked away I notice him still rubbing his leg and cursing. Why not just step on the thing? Why not just throw it on the tracks? Why put a lit cigarette in your pocket? People do the damndest things. It's not my leg, so what the hell. There's more out there for me to see.

Let's move on through the escapades of being in the belly of the beast, which are the subways of New York. As I progressed in my learning on the job, my tendencies of talking to and approaching the public improved. I went from being just a station-to-station cop, to a train patrol cop. Moving under the city in a northbound southbound shuffle.

▼

SUMMER LOVE

One Sunday afternoon while doing train patrol headed for Pelham Bay, the last stop of a one-hour trip each way, I watched as the passengers moved from the rear of the train to the lead car to exit. As this was the closest point to quickly get off the Iron Beast. The faster you got off the train the better you felt, made another trip without being mugged. I could tell the relief on the faces of the people as they all crammed into the lead car. Thank God it's almost over.

I assumed all the passengers on the train were now in this car but I decided to do a walk through just to make sure. As I sailed through the empty cars I felt good. No drunks, nobody sleeping and no crime. This was too good to be true. Into the car before the last, no lights, damn, watch my step. Check the conductor's cabs with the switches to make sure no one has been playing with them. Luck still holding, just an electrical problem. Keep moving just one car to go. As I peer into the last car from the darkness I see a young male and female sitting and snuggling, how cute.

The couple unaware of my presence goes about their business of petting. As the passion moves through the young man he releases his love embrace upon the girl. He starts to look around, head moving from left to right. Yeah, I know this action. He's up to something. With a quick glance he stares toward the car in which I am watching from but he doesn't see me.

After a moment the young man stands up. Reaching down for his love he takes her hand and draws her to him, kissing her passionately. He then spins her around. She must be thinking, "What is he doing?" The young man then places the female in a leaning position with her hands pressed against the seat of the train.

Again he looks around. I'm still there, unknown to the young Romeo. He reaches down under the skirt of his beloved, lifts her skirt and then goes for his zipper. He must be crazy. She must be crazy. I know they have better sense than to do what I think they are going to do.

Wrong, with a quick lunge forward the act of lovemaking has began. Both of them lost in their desire to please go about their lovemaking in a wild and consuming way, for all of three minutes. It's over. They kiss, fix their clothing and sit.

Now I enter their car, glance down towards them not speaking, just going about my business. To the rear of the car I move, everything looks fine. I turn towards the couple. They both smile at me. Knowing what they have just done. Having sex on a subway train. Almost being caught by a cop. They must feel great.

As I walk pass the couple again, I turn stating, "I saw what you were doing in here." A wave of my hand gestures the young man to his feet. "What were you thinking, how old are you?" "Eighteen, Sir." How old is she? "Eighteen, Sir." Holding back laughter I go into police mode, "Give me some ID, both of you. I should put you both under the jail. Why couldn't you wait till you got home?" With this question the young man handing me a fist full of papers reply, "We are married. We got married two weeks ago, look at the papers I gave you." Well what do you know they are married. But why do the wild thing on a subway train. I must know.

The young man stated, "We live with her family, mother, father and brother. We share a bedroom with her brother. We have no private time to ourselves. The family is always home. Not one chance to do what a husband and wife do. We could not wait anymore. We're sorry. You married? Then you know what I mean. We just had to." "Stop, Stop," I said, "I understand your problem but the subway is not the place. Why not go to a hotel or some motel? You must be kidding me, I should take you both in."

The young woman starts to cry. The young man panics. Not knowing what to say, out of his mouth comes, "Look, I don't mind, you can..." halting his speech, "you can...you know," while motioning to his bride. She is looking up at me, eyes blinking and smiling while nodding yes with her head. I spit out, "I can what?! You both are crazy, what the hell you mean I can..." not knowing whether to laugh or pull out the cuffs.

I think if I take this into the command I'll never hear the end of it. Why me, the day was going along so well. Let's see, they are married, they have the proof. I do have discretion, it's not like they killed someone. With that my mine is made up, "Get up, get up, take your papers and get away from me. Let's go. Get off this train." The couple excited that they are not going to be arrested, head towards the lead car and freedom. Thanking me all the way for being so kind. "Shut up," I say, "Just keep moving."

As we reach the lead car all the other passengers have left the train. The conductor wonders where we came from. He hears me state to the couple, "Get a room," as they leave. As I related the story of what happened to the conductor he looks stunned. Then quips, "I guess it's good you are the cop and not me because I would have torn that ass up, while grabbing his crotch area and laughing. Damn you let that shit go, you must be the stupid one," "No," I reply, "Just doing my job. They are young and in love, been there myself, but you are a pervert."

Later that day while having a cup of coffee I thought to myself if I tell people about this, they will say I am lying. I tell you, you cannot make this stuff up. If I didn't see it for myself, I wouldn't believe it either.

CHAPTER 4

▼

THE LIGHT OF LOVE

Maybe it's the weather, the hot blistering days of summer, the longing to be wanted, the need to be with another or maybe it's the subway I don't know. But whatever it is in the dark lonely spaces of the system all the pent up feelings seem to come out of people. Take for example one Sunday afternoon. The temperature outside was about ninety degrees. The temperature in the hole seemed to be over one hundred degrees.

The day seems to be going along well. Looking forward to mealtime, get off my feet, just to sit. Oh how good it was going to be. I step off the train at the 167th street station. The station was dark only one person a male sitting on the bench. The idea of sitting down takes up most of my thoughts. Food, yes food, what should I get? Anything would be great at this point.

As I approach the man on the bench I realize that he is talking to himself, nothing new for the subway. I nod, how are you? No response, later for him. As I walk by I notice something wet on the ground it's a dark liquid. I think soda, coffee, who cares. I'm going for food. Just about this time a train starts to enter the station. I stop to wait for the passengers, if any, to get off. As the train begins to enter, the man gets up from the bench. He's about eight feet away from me. He yells out, "I don't want to live" and heads for the edge of the platform.

Shit, no not now. "What the hell is he doing," flashes in my head. I run to stop him before he jumps. Grabbing the man I pull him back to the bench and make him sit. Asking him, "What the hell is your problem," while holding him down. I feel something wet on his clothing. A look at my hands and I see blood. Blood on me, blood on the bench, blood on the ground. Not soda, not coffee, but blood. Is it mine? No, it must be his but from where.

The man is still talking out of his head, asking me to let him die. Quick with the cuffs, on they go. A check of the man reveals that the blood is coming from his rear. The butt of his pants is soaked. I call for an ambulance. "Question, what happened to you? Who did this to you?" For a moment I'm thinking I got a victim of a crime, not a person that wants to kill himself. Over the radio I say, "Central I have a male, stabbed, bleeding badly, perpetrator unknown, send backup." Again I question, "What happened to you?"

By now you should have guessed that the answer was not going to be a normal one, and it wasn't. Standing and listening in disbelief at what this person is telling me. I wonder what the hell is wrong with the people in this city. What the hell is wrong with the world? For the answer that I was being given did not want to register in my brain.

"I had a fight with my boyfriend," the man states. "We had broken up. Last night I saw him and tried to get back with him. We had some drinks and then went back to my apartment where I rocked his world. I did everything for him. I wanted him to want me. When I finished making love to him, he said, 'I got something special for you.' He turned me on my stomach and began to rub and kiss me all over. Then he poured baby oil on me and took out a tubular light bulb. Passing the light bulb up and down my body while entering me with his fingers. Suddenly he placed the bulb inside of me and asked how does that feel. It was great. He kept this up for a few moments, then I heard him say, 'Didn't I tell you I didn't want you anymore.' With that while the bulb was still inside of me he raised his hand and slammed my ass checks together, breaking the bulb inside of me. I screamed. He laughed, grabbed his clothing while cursing me out he left me there. I tried to stop the bleeding but I couldn't."

"He broke a light bulb in your ass!" I said, "What the fuck is that, what the hell was he thinking, why didn't you go to the hospital?" "I don't know," he said, "I needed to find him. I love him. I need him. I've been looking for him all night."

The ambulance arrives. I tell the medic what the situation is. He looks at me like I got two heads or something. I say, "It's true." The man is placed face down on a stretcher and they cut away his pants. The sight of his butt was like nothing I had ever seen before. There in front of me was a human butt, the butt-hole about the size of a silver dollar, cuts all around it with the blood still flowing. The medic spots something else. There is a fist full of toilet paper inserted inside of the man's butt. He pulls it out. Damn the sight of this bloody mess is ruining my appetite. The medic states to the man, "What's this?"

The man said that before he left to look for his lover, he unrolled a roll of toilet paper. He then rolled it up smaller and inserted it into his butt to try and stop the bleeding, but it didn't work. The medic and I stare at each other. He then tries to remove pieces of glass that are sticking out of the man's butt. The man grunts and yells. When the rest of the cops arrived, I related to them what the condition was. They laugh at me and leave.

The Sergeant sends me to the hospital with the man. As I sit in the emergency room waiting for this man to be treated and logged in as an emotionally disturbed person, my stomach growls. I think well, you'll eat when you get home. Wait till I tell my wife about this one. She'll say I'm lying. Who wouldn't, but it's true. The whole damn thing is true. I don't know what happened to the man after I left him at the hospital. But I know one thing, you can't make this stuff up, not even Steven King could come up with this stuff.

CHAPTER 5

▼

THE VEGETARIAN

Staying with the subway love or should that be lust topic let's go back to the 86th and Lexington Avenue station. This was really one for the hall of fame. A hectic day had come to a low. Not too many people, the tour coming to an end. Just waiting for that go-home train. It's about ten o'clock at night no one on station but the clerk and I. The station is quiet. It's all I could ask for. Take another walk around, nothing. Cross over to the northbound side to wait for train. Clerk almost asleep. This is good or so it seemed.

Then the cleaner comes from around the corner, waves me to come over. I think, now what? He says, "I don't know but I think there's something going on in the females toilet." "Like what?" I asked. "I don't know," said the cleaner, "But you better take a look." This is all I need. Getting ready to go home, now I got to step into some shit. Over to the toilet, slowly, listening for any sound. Watching for any kind of movement, nothing. What's the cleaner talking about?

Then I hear it, a low moan coming from inside of the toilet. The moan gets louder, stronger. I reach for my gun. Gripping it tightly in my hand. Back against the wall, sliding across slowly, slowly up to the door. The thought of rape in progress flashes in my mine. How do I handle this, should I call for backup, should I just rush in, what should I do?

Got to do something. Turn radio down, get tighter grip on gun. No, don't call for back up yet. You don't know what you got. I say to myself, "You don't want to look like a fool if it's something stupid." Ok, I got to go in. Should I announce myself? No, don't want to give up my advantage of surprise. Through the door I go, slowly. The moans are really loud, coming from the second stall. Check the room. No one is visible. Look under the stalls, feet, only one pair, in the second stall.

I make my way into the first stall. I step up on the toilet. Alright this is a good position. Take a deep breath. It's now or never. I reach up to pull myself to the top of the wall separating the stalls. Now quickly, thrust the gun over and get sights lined up. "Police don't move!" I yell. A scream cuts the air. My eyes focus on the person. It's a woman, one woman, but not just any woman. She's a skell, what we call the homeless, a skell with a large zucchini, about two feet in length with a curve in it.

"What the hell you doing in the ladies room, get out of here," she says. My eyes are wide open. My brain does not want to register what I am seeing, but it's true. I am really seeing this. A female skell with a zucchini inserted into her vagina. Having sex with it and from the sounds she was making, good sex. She screams again, "Get the fuck out of here. Help, police, help!"

Gathering myself, I let fly with the mouth, "You must be kidding me. What the hell are you doing?" I jumped down from my perch. She slams open the stall door, zucchini in hand, covered with her fluids and damn the smell that came from her. I cannot even describe the smell. Again I stated, "Get yourself together and get out of here." While stepping out the door and placing my gun back into its holster.

The look of shock that must have been on my face stunned the cleaner. He was looking at me in anticipation, waiting for me to tell him what I had found. I almost could not speak but out came the words, "You aren't going to believe this. I can't believe what I saw." "What? Tell me what did you see, what happened in there?" he asked.

Before I could speak, out comes the female. Still cursing, carrying two shopping bags filled with her worldly possessions, zucchini sticking out from one of the bags. She blasts at me, "You ain't suppose to come into the ladies room. Someone should kick your ass, you bastard." "Get out of here," I shot back, "Get off my station." She turns and proceeds to exit the station. The cleaner, still wanting to know what had happened, pressed me for information.

When I told him what I had witnessed he said I was lying, no way could that be true. He had seen things on the subway before also but never anything like what I had told him. He says to me, "Now I bet you've seen it all." I thought to myself I hope so, but deep down inside I knew there would be other sights more stranger than this, more unbelievable. When I would see them I didn't know.

What I would see? I didn't know, but I knew there were more out there for me to witness. All I had to do was keep my eyes open.

CHAPTER 6

▼

SHOES

The lonely nights in the subway sometimes could get to me. Fixed at one station for eight hours, one station no longer than two football fields. Fixed on a midnight to eight tour. Fixed at Bleeker street. I don't know if you have ever been to the Bleeker street subway station, but it's not a pretty sight. No people not even a clerk on the overnight tour. The booth closed. Only the northbound platform for me, no southbound, I am fixed on this platform for eight hours.

For some reason the department thinks by me walking up and down this one platform all night that the people of the area will feel safe. Ok, maybe it sounds good except for one thing. There are no people. The trains come in. No one gets off. Not a soul enters the station. What the hell am I doing here?

As the night moves along, it must be about two or three o'clock now. Look at watch, shit it's only twelve-thirty. I've only been here for forty-five minutes. Lord help me. This is not going to be a good night. Find a position on the wall to lean. Ok, this feels good. I'll lean here for a while. Look up and down the platform. Nothing. Look onto the track area. "What's that?"

I see a pair of brown shoes, just the tips sticking out from behind one of the columns. Don't see a person in them, just the shoes. Someone must have thrown them on the tracks I think. Take a walk down to the end of my home for the night. Then back to my leaning position. Stay awake, must stay awake. My eyes make their way back to the track area.

Where are the shoes? They moved. The shoes moved. They must have moved ten feet or more. Still behind a column, but not the same column. Hey, there must be someone in those shoes. "Yo, hey you," I called out, "Get off the tracks."

No answer. No movement. I take out my flashlight. Shine it on the shoes, still nothing. I call again, again no response. I cannot see anyone. All I can see are the shoes. Up the stairs over to the southbound side I go. If someone is hiding behind that column I'll see them from the southbound side. Open the gate with my key, onto the platform, over to the spot where the shoes are.

Wait a minute. The shoes have moved again. Same spot. But now they are on the other side of the column. "Hey you, "I yelled, "I told you to get off the tracks." No answer. I watch. A train rips past the station. The motorman didn't blow his horn. He had to see the guy. Why didn't he blow his horn? Ok up the stairs, back to the northbound side, down the platform. Where are the shoes? I don't see them. I walk down a little further, there they are, but back on the southbound side of the column. Someone is playing with me.

Another train cuts through the station, again the motorman doesn't blow his horn. Maybe the draft from the train, I think, is moving the shoes. Yeah, that's what's happening, but how come they don't flip over, or fly out from behind the column. They just moved a couple of feet but are still upright, from one side of the column to the other. Alright lets see what happens when this train clears the station. If the draft of the train is moving them, then they should move now.

The train clears. My eyes zoom in on the shoes. They are in the same spot, didn't move, now what. I know, I'll just stand here and watch. If someone is in those shoes, they will have to move sooner or later, I got all night. Ten minutes, nothing. Thirty minutes, no movement. Four trains have passed by and nothing. No horns, no change in the position of the shoes.

Alright I had enough. Up the stairs, over to the southbound side, I got to see what's up with those shoes. Key my way into the station on the southbound side, down the platform, where are they. Where are they? Damn, they moved again. No train had passed by while I was crossing over. I still cannot see anyone in the shoes. Quickly back over to the northbound side. Where are they? Shit they moved again.

This is not funny anymore something strange is going on here. The column is still blocking my view of any person in the shoes. I can see the shoes but I can't see any person in them. But there has to be someone in them. Know what, I'm not going to move. I'm going to stare at those shoes until I see who's in them.

After another fifteen minutes of staring at the shoes I must relax my eyes. Blinking them hard, trying to clear them. I get ready for another round. Back to the shoes, where are they? They moved, I only looked away for a second, where are they? There they are, still on the tracks but about fifty feet from where I last saw them. I had heard nothing. I had seen nothing. What's going on here?

This time keep your eyes open. Don't blink. Don't move your eyes. Stay fixed on the shoes. Eyes starting to blur, must take a break. Look away for a second, back to the shoes. You guessed it, they moved. This time almost all the way to the end of the station, about two feet away from the tunnel entrance, still on the southbound side of the column. I head down towards the end where the shoes are. Walking swiftly, I got to see. At the entrance to the tunnel there are no columns. Once the shoes move past the column they are behind now, I got him or her.

As I reach the end of the platform I am amazed. The shoes are gone. I didn't see them move. Where did they go? A chill runs up my spine. I stare into the darkness. What the hell is going on here? Forget it. Let it go, must have been a skell fucking with me, I hoped. The night is almost over. I board my go home train still thinking about those shoes, just cannot get them out of my mind.

As the train leaves the station, I watch the platform. Clear, looks good, nothing happening. Then all of a sudden, there are the shoes outside the gate. Still can't see anyone in them. How did they get there? The gates locked, the only way to get in there is with a key. I was standing in that area before I boarded the train. I didn't hear the chain on the gates. I didn't see anyone climb up from the tracks. That area was clear. What the hell is happening? Forget it, put it out of your mind. Whatever it was, who ever it was it's gone now. Its over, go home and forget it, I wish it were that easy. To this day I still don't know what I witnessed that night, all I know is that I didn't see anyone in those shoes.

CHAPTER 7

▼

SLICE OF LIFE

Enough with all of this light stuff. Lets get to some other sights that the normal New Yorker never gets to see. Now I must warn those of you that some of the visions that you are going to read from this point on may not be for the weak. These are not bedtime stories. No, these are true visions from the subways of New York. Are you ready? Clean your glasses or refresh your contacts because the next few tales will keep your eyes glued to these pages. Remember you were warned.

Well, I made it through the summer, a hot sticky summer. It seems like there was something new everyday, a new surprise around almost every corner. I understood that the things that I was coming across were making me a better cop and also a better person. Just by being involved in such natural and unnatural adventures were expanding me to new heights. You know I really do like my job.

Here it is another day in the subway. Another day of northbound, southbound, upstairs, downstairs, listening to the snide remarks of my adoring public. Remarks like, "What you couldn't be a real cop, so you took this job instead," or, "Do you guys carry guns?" But my favorite had to be, "Excuse me, I need you to call the police for me." When I responded, "I am the police." A look of disbelief would come across the face of the person, who would then speak, "You're a transit guard I need a real cop, not a toy cop."

Most of the time after such a conversation, the person would just walk away. Which kept a lot of crap from coming my way. Sometimes I didn't need to get involved in a tit for tat, to pick up crap. A lot of the time all I had to do was just step into a train or onto a platform. Stepping into shit is how the cops would refer to these encounters.

Take the night at Bedford Park station. Again nothing is happening just sweat, sweat in October. The city is cooling down but the subway is still cooking at about ninety degrees or more. Alright enough with this reminiscing, lets get to the good stuff.

I step into a southbound "C" train. A quick look around the car, it looks ok. Except for some drunk sitting on the floor next to the storm door leading to the next car. Ok, let me make an entry in my little black book that I got on this train, then I'll go and wake him up. He's sleeping, there's no rush.

Entry completed, adjust hat, got to look good. There's maybe eight or nine people sitting in this car all going about their personal business, reading the paper, listening to tapes through headsets, or sleeping, whatever. Whatever it took to block out anyone that may want to invade their space, especially me.

The drunk is still sitting next to the door. As I get closer to him I could see that the storm door was sliding back and forth with the rocking of the train. The door was bouncing off of the person's chest. With his legs inside of the car, his head and right shoulder leaning out between the cars, I'm thinking this guy is really out of it, that door has got to hurt.

I tap him on his left shoulder, no response. I tug on his shoulder, no response. I step back and put on my gloves. Looks like I'm going to need a good grip because this guy is not moving. Don't want to use too much force, just enough to get this guy to move.

I look around at my public, knowing now that all eyes would be on me. "Excuse me sir, excuse me sir, you alright? You got to get up." Still nothing. No movement, no sound. I get a good grip on his shoulder. Now with one swift pull, I bring this drunk all the way into the car. I wish that was all I did but no.

With that pull not only did I remove the drunk from the door entrance but I also removed what was remaining of his brain from his body. See, what I didn't expect was to be covered from head to waist with blood, brain matter and stuff from inside of a human body that I cannot even describe, with that the train car jumped to life.

Yeah we got a show now. "Damn look at that guy, did the cop do that to him, someone yelled." Spitting out what ever it was that flew into my mouth, I heard myself yelling, "Oh shit, what the hell, what the hell happened to you?" As if the guy could answer. You see he only had half of his head, from the eyebrows up was gone, sliced off. What was being held inside by the missing portion was now slid-ing down my uniform or across the floor of the train.

Out comes the radio. The call is placed that I have a D/O/A on a southbound "C" coming into Tremont Avenue. One of the passengers ran to tell the conduc-tor what was happening. As the train came to a halting stop, I slipped in the humanity under my feet, hitting the floor of the train. I'm now fully covered in blood. It looks like the inside of a slaughterhouse in here. This guy's got no head. The complete top of his head is gone. He looks like some kind of cartoon. Get-ting to my feet I step off the train and wait for help. I'm not touching this guy again, not on your life.

The mystery of what happened to this guy didn't take long for the detectives to solve. Turns out the guy was riding between the cars of the train, when he stuck his head up to get a look over the top of the train. When wham! A support beam inside of the tunnel came to say hello and goodbye all in one quick slicing pass.

I knew this guy was dead, a life lost and the only thing that I could think about was how I had to buy a new uniform, cause I ain't wearing this one again. No matter how many times my wife washes it. Damn, that's about a hundred dollars out of my pocket because this guy wanted to fuck around on the subway. I think I'm beginning to get immune to stuff like this happening, callous, tough skin. I need it, to finish out my career I need it.

CHAPTER 8

▼

HEAD BANGER

People losing their heads in the subway seem almost to be norm, maybe one or two a week. That brings to mind rush hour at the 149th street station. Now this station really rocks. You got the college at the top of the stairs and the students are always trying to get over. So it keeps me on my toes, alert and ready for action. 149th street is a major transfer point. People everywhere, jammed in two or three deep. It's six o'clock. I'm watching the trains enter and leave, watching for people riding between the cars or exiting between the cars. This is an easy summons and besides that, I don't need another headless horseman.

A young man is saying goodbye to his friends, handshaking, backslapping, bumping of the forearms the manly way to part. I watched as the young man boarded the northbound train. He opens up a side window of the train and continues talking to his buddies. Now he leans his head out of the window, still yapping to his crew. The doors close. The train starts to move. This guy is still yapping away. The train is going northbound and he's looking southbound with his head still out the window.

The train is picking up speed. The young man's buddies yell for him to get in the train. I start running towards the train also yelling for him to get his head inside of the train. Making my way down the platform was not easy. The people just refused to get out of my way, this is New York and they do have rights. I was losing ground on the train but still yelling as loud as I could, "Get in the train."

With a look of defiance on his face and curses firing out of his mouth the young man paid me no attention, not knowing that his life would soon be over.

As the train entered the tunnel, the sound of human bone crashing into the cement was booming. Splat!! The white tiles leading to the entrance are now stained a bright red. Someone pulls the emergency cord and the train comes to a stop. I boarded the train from the rear and made my way to where the body was. The body of this young man that only moments ago was alive, alive and cursing at me for trying to save his life. There he was slumped on the floor, washed in blood. The inside of the train looks like a Picasso painting. There's something missing though. His head is gone.

The search for this guy's head takes two hours. No one could find it, not on the train, not under the train. It hit the wall but no way could his head just disintegrate into nothing. Emergency Rescue is looking. I'm looking. There must be twenty cops and firemen looking for this guy's head. Where the hell could it be? Finally, after all the time we spent searching the northbound end of the station, comes a call of, "I got it, I got the head," from a cop about halfway down the southbound tracks.

I'm thinking, he must be kidding. That's about two hundred feet away and on the other side of the station. Anyway I go to take a look. The cop bends down reaches with his left hand and pulls up the head by the hair. There were no eyes. The back of the head was completely flat. I watched in disbelief as the cop walks over to the platform still holding the head, while calling out, "I got it, I got the head, that was some bank shot." Playing in the subway is not a good idea, those trains are too big and they never lose.

CHAPTER 9

▼

WHERE IS IT?

Over the years the Bronx seemed to be wearing on me. Time to move to another part of the city. Maybe the sights and the people would be different. Hello Queens! Yes, Queens, a cleaner, quieter place, I hoped. A slower pace, a nicer group of citizens, at least this is what I thought. No such luck. People are people, no matter where you go. The streets maybe cleaner, the citizens may dress nicer and the buildings aren't falling down. There are more private homes, mostly kept up, but looks can be deceiving. People are people, nothing changed just because I left one borough for another.

My first day of working in Queens is a day tour. Feels good to be seeing new people, new sights, a breath of fresh air. Out of the command, heading to post, a call comes over the radio of a person walking on the tracks between Queens Borough Plaza and Court House Square on the #7 line. The #7 line is an elevated outside line that runs from Main Street in Flushing to Grand Central Station in Manhattan. "10/4 Central, I'll check and advise," is the response that I gave. Making my way through the train, I asked the radio operator if the Transit Authority had been notified of the person on the tracks. "Standby unit," I'm told, "I'll check."

Now this #7 train that I'm in is really moving. Picking up speed with no intention of slowing down. The morning rush hour is still going on, so the trains got to run fast and on time. Still squeezing pass the passengers crammed into each car, I'm getting closer to the motorman. Got to get to him to make sure he knows about the person on the tracks. "Central any update from the Transit Authority?" I asked. "Unit, be advised that the trains have been cautioned in that area." This meant that the trains are still running but are supposed to be going slow, looking for this person. "10/4" is my answer.

As my train is leaving Queens Borough Plaza, Wham! The breaks lock up, people falling everywhere. The conductor is heard on the speaker asking, "What happened is everything alright up front?" No answer from the motorman. That oh-shit feeling is running all through my body. Not on my first day out here, not now, it's too early in the morning for this. I didn't even have my second cup of coffee yet.

Up to the lead car I go. The motorman is out on the tracks looking under the train. I hear him say, "Shit! Shit! Where did he come from?" That's right the train had run someone over. Here we go again. Emergency Rescue, the Duty Captain, the Detectives, the Sergeant, everybody and their mama were on the way.

The passengers seem to be taking things well. Who am I kidding? They were pissed. If this guy wasn't already dead they would have killed him for stopping the train and making them late for whatever business or appointment that had them going into the city. "How dare this guy get hit by their train, why couldn't the next one have killed him?" This is what most, if not all, the passengers were thinking.

Remember, this is New York and as wrong as it may sound even though no one had the nerve to say it, this is how they most likely felt. I could tell by the looks on their faces.

Also I could tell by the questions that were asked. "How long before we're going to move?" "I don't know, someone was hit by the train so it's going be a while," I responded. "That's just great. We're fucked now, this shits going to take all day," was the heartfelt comments from the 'concerned' passengers.

Well, Emergency Rescue got the guy out from under the train in record time but there was just one little problem, he had no head. The body was pretty much intact, not too many cuts. Not even his clothing was that dirty. Looking down at the body if you didn't know this guy had no head you might think he was just sleeping. That sounds familiar.

The search under the train turns up nothing, the search of the tracks nothing, a search of the street area under the tracks, no head. The only thing left to do was for the crew to take the train to the train yard and give it a good going over.

Me, I'm on my way to the morgue again. Seems like I'm here once a month or more. The morgue guy calls me to come inside of his work area. Sure why not, been there, done that, he can't freak me out. Question he asked, "I know he was hit by a train, but where's his head?" "I don't know," I say, "We couldn't find it." "Alright lets see what we got here," the morgue guy says. Raising a sharp knife he moves his hand over the chest area of the headless man. He began to cut. No screw this. I'm getting out of here. "I'll be outside," I say. "Chicken," is what I hear next. "Say what you want but I'm leaving."

About thirty minutes crawls by, here comes the morgue guy, carrying some x-rays and sort of joking with another morgue employee in the hallway. They look at me sitting in the office and smile. Something's up, what could it be? Well, the search for the head would come to an end, for the mystery had been solved.

Looking at the x-ray it was hard to believe my eyes, but there it was in black and white, right in front of me. The head I could see it, pushed down inside of the chest cavity of the guy, I mean jammed deep inside of himself. The force of the train hitting him was so powerful that it caved his head into his chest. The morgue guy said that he must have been walking with his head hung down when the train hit him. He took the full force of the train on the top of his head causing it to be driven into his chest. Now that's weird.

CHAPTER 10

▼

TRAPPED

As the Christmas season approaches the city seems to be all aglow with people smiling, being nicer than usual, walking around with shopping bags full of presents on Union Turnpike, not a big shopping area, but still a busy station. I'm on meal at Nathan's, hot dogs and soda, French fries and apple pie, now that's eating. A call comes over the radio of a train that has gone into emergency while leaving the station. Meal over got to go.

Entering the station I see people crying, others just standing around staring, not speaking but pointing me towards the front of the train. As I stroll down the platform I have to watch my step, as there is some sort of strange looking substance on the ground. There's the motorman coming out from between the train and the wall, he looks pretty cocky. "Must have hit some trash on the roadbed," I'm thinking. "Yeah we got one," he says, "Between the seventh and eighth cars." The same old routine again, Emergency Rescue, Duty Captain. Enough! Everybody and their mama are in route to the station. I must find out if anyone witnessed what happened.

I'm in luck, not only do I have a witness, I have thirty people that saw how this person came to be mangled by a southbound "E" train. All the stories were the same. As the doors of the train closed, a woman was seen running down the stairs. She was carrying two shopping bags in her left hand and had a shoulder bag slung over her neck and right shoulder. With one motion she swung her shoulder bag between the doors, hoping to make them reopen as they closed in on her bag. No such luck.

The door did not reopen. As the train began to move, the woman trapped by her strap that was around her neck, bangs on the door, pleading for help. With the train picking up speed passengers inside were trying feverishly to free the trapped woman. They tried pulling the doors apart while yelling out to her to let go of the bag. ,

Oh, if only she could. The shoulder bag filled with Christmas joy is just too big for the passengers to push through the small opening that they managed to create. The woman, fear in her eyes, feet moving as fast as possible, she lost her balance while being dragged along the platform by the train. For some reason no one pulled the emergency cord to stop the train. No one had thought about it. Her head hitting the platform, flesh being torn from her body, the tunnel was approaching fast, to late. The wall is here, bang, rip, snap, she's gone.

The foreign substance that I had been stepping over on the platform turned out to be brain matter, and pieces of skull. As the train is moved out for her body to be recovered, now the full extent of damage could be seen. If I was not told that this was a woman, if I was not told that this was once a human, I would not have known what it was. Now I had seen people that were hit by trains before, but I had never seen a person torn into so many pieces.

A leg over here, a leg over there, internal organs lying all over the tracks, torso split in two, arms ripped from the sockets. This poor woman was removed with shovels, just lumped into a big black bag, scooped up and dumped into the back of an ambulance.

Remember, I was told that this woman had two shopping bags when she came down the stairs. Well I never found them, with all the confusion, and the attempt of the passengers to save this women's life, some enterprising person took the opportunity to help himself to her presents. Maybe that person thought, what use are they to her now? She has no use for them, Finder's keeper. Remember this is New York.

▼

CHAPTER 11

THE WATCHER

The subway is full of blood and you never know when another drop will be spilt. A young man is seen pacing back and forth on the end of the Parson's Blvd. station. As the Manhattan bound "F" train begins to enter the station the young man throws himself in front of it. Not one word was heard from him, no warning before his leap to death.

When someone dies in the subway and the blood is flowing, the smell hangs in the air. Once you smell it you never forget it. The general public doesn't know that smell. They smell something but don't know that it is the smell of death.

When this young man is removed from under the train he's cut into two pieces, cut clean through at the waist. His wounds were sealed by the heat created from the wheels of the train, not too much bleeding, a clean cut.

This time I'm only assisting, thank God. Let some other cop handle this. I've had my share. A rookie is watching as the post cop conducts a search of the young man for ID and any other personal effects. When the young man was removed from under the train and placed onto the platform, he was placed face up with his lower portion and upper torso touching in the middle, the look was as if he was still intact, still whole. As the officer is going about the body search, the rookie is leaning over his shoulder, trying to see everything.

Excited by what is taking place the sweat is pouring down from beneath his hat. A drop hits the officer conducting the search on the back of his neck. Turning to the rookie he tells him to back off. No use, the rookie is locked into this scene and he doesn't want to miss anything. Again sweat falls onto the back of the searching officer's neck. He gives a look to me out the corner of his eye. He winks at me. I'm like, what's he up to?

Before I know it the officer reaches down and grabs the young man's belt buckle, getting a firm grip he proceeds to pull up, as he does this the two parts separate. The wounds that had been sealed are now open. Intestines, and other internal organs are now visible, the blood is starting to flow and the smell is getting stronger.

Well the rookie got more than he bargained for, because as the scene grew more gross, his lunch, breakfast and maybe even last nights dinner came back to pay him a visit. That was the most disgusting thing that I had seen in a long time, not the blood, not the guts, but the vomit. What the hell did that rookie eat?!

Yes, the visions were still coming. The visions were all around me, there was no getting away from them. For as long as I was to remain in the subway the more visions I would come to see. By now I wanted to see more because each new vision seem to be getting more and more intense. I must see more. I must.

▼

A TAXING SITUATION

Now by me telling you the visions that have passed before my eyes, I do not want to scare anyone into not riding the subway again. My intent is to inform you of the dangers that lurk. To let you know the possibility of meeting a quick and maybe painful end under the wheels of a cold non-caring killer, the subway. The visions of mangled and chewed up human flesh is not a pretty one but one seen more often than the regular New Yorker can imagine.

Our next vision will take us to the 75th Avenue station, a local stop on the "F" and "G" line. This is a very quiet station. A station where anyone could take time to think or to just let their mind wander. Not a lot of people milling about to distract one from enjoying a moment of quiet time. It's tax day. People rushing to file that last minute tax return. Not me, I get my papers in the mail as quick as possible. A cop in New York doesn't make enough to start with. Screw waiting to file a return, I need my money now.

Here comes the call, "All units be advised, coming from the train crew, report of man under, southbound 75th Ave. Any unit to check and advise?" I'm at the Van Wyck Blvd. station two stops away, but it's impossible for me to get to 75th Ave. via train because the train with the man under it is blocking the tunnel.

I run up to the street looking for any sort of transportation. Luck is with me. A patrol car comes blaring down Queens Blvd. They stop and pick me up, shouting, "Lets go!" I jump into the rear seat and away we fly. Weaving in and out of traffic we arrive at 75th Ave. within two minutes.

We rush down the stairs. Passengers from the disabled train are pointing the way. Some know what's going on, some don't. Reaching the platform I see the motorman and conductor aboard the now empty train.

The motorman is sitting holding his head in his hands. The conductor has his right hand on the left shoulder of the motorman. As I step through the door of the train I hear the conductor say, "It's not your fault, what could you do?" I realize that the motorman is crying uncontrollably.

I motion to the conductor to come over to me. "Where is he, where's the man under?" We walk three cars back, out comes the flashlight. "Look there," says the conductor. Inbetween the third and fourth cars I could see the figure of a person, twisted and bent. "Central, be advised it's confirmed, we do have someone under the train."

There's nothing that can be done, it's obvious that this person is dead. Back to the motorman I go. Looking at the motorman, seeing him fall apart, hands shaking, tears flowing down his cheeks, I really didn't want to ask him any questions, but I had to. Choosing the right words I started with the standard, "Can you tell me what happened?" Slowly, gathering his thoughts the motorman began to speak. "He jumped, the motherfucker jumped! Just as we entered the station, he looked right at me, then he jumped, why me, why did he have to do this to me?"

The troops landed, swarming all over the station. Most of the guys are just trying to get a look at the body, but it's no use, he's wedged under the train, out of sight. Finally after what felt like hours but in reality only thirty minutes had passed, the body is removed from the tracks. Left arm, left leg, right arm, thrown onto the platform. Next comes the rest of what used to be a living, breathing human.

The train is moved out of the station and the shovels are brought in. Scoop by scoop what's left from the inside of the unlucky soul is dumped into a black hefty bag. The station cleaner pours bleach on the red mess left behind. It's sanitation at its best.

A search of the bloody pants worn by this mauled mass of flesh turns up an envelope. It contained a tax return for the former hardworking man. A closer look at the papers revealed the identity of the man and it also gave a clue as to why he had jumped into the path of the steel wheels of death. Now we have all heard the saying, "Nothing is certain in life but death and taxes." Well from what was on those papers this guy owed the IRS more than two hundred thousand dollars. His wages were being garnisheed his house had been seized and his bank account was frozen. He had lost everything.

I cannot even imagine what he was feeling as he stood on that platform. The torture of trying to come up with a solution to his problem must have been eating him up inside. How could he make things right, how? Once such a large sum is owed to the government it's impossible for the average person to make it right. For this man the only answer was death. The taxes were for certain so the death had to follow. More, you want more...

CHAPTER 13

▼

RAIN MAN

Well I got another little tale for you. A bright sunny spring day I'm outside. Out of the hole on an elevated station. Fresh air. Yes, sweet fresh air. With the sun beating down it's time to work on my tan. The day is just perfect. Got a few tickets, that'll keep the Sergeant off my back for a few days. The Mets are playing and believe it or not, they are winning, a New York miracle. Soon the crowds would be filling the stations. Everyone is in place anticipating the swarms of jolly fans to come.

Then it happens, the call, "Man under Junction Blvd. southbound #7." Arriving at the station, I am met by loads of people all yelling in Spanish. I have no idea what they are saying. Women are crying, men are angry. A young girl comes over to me, I asked, "Did you see what happened?" "Yes," she says.

Before she could finish, I interrupted her, asking "Why are those guys so angry?" The young girl in her broken English tells me, "That guy, that guy up there under the train, he robbed the store over there," while pointing to some spot across the street. "Ok, then what?" I asked. "Well, he rob the store and some other guys chase him. He run up here and they still chase him. He run to try and go to the other side when he get hit, that's all. Those guys over there didn't do nothing."

Well let me make sure that you know that we are on an elevated station. There is no solid track area. The trains run on rails that open to the ground below.

Which means that the street area is visible from the station platforms. The station is roped off and the street under the station is roped off as well.

There is one strange sight. A black convertible is also roped off, why? Don't laugh. This is serious. It seems that when the train struck the robber, the convertible was stopped at a traffic light, with its top down. The driver had no clue of what was about to be deposited in his car. As the southbound #7 train tore through the different parts of the unlucky robber's body, they began to rain down onto Roosevelt Ave. Not your regular rain, the rain of human body parts. Pieces of the robber littered the car from front to rear.

The owner of the car stood on the street corner, shocked, covered in blood. Only a portion of the robbers frame and it's former contents were recovered on the station. The rest of him was located in the convertible. The Crime Scene Unit finished up their business, taking pictures, gathering information and sorting through all the details. Body removed, train sent on its way, only one thing left to do.

"Hey guy," calls the Crime Scene Detective over to the owner of the car. "You can have it now, we're finished." The owner of the car looks even more shocked, "What the hell you mean you're finished! Look at my car, who's going to clean up my car?" "Beats me," says the detective, "That's not our problem." With this the owner loses all control. Cursing and waving his arms, he cannot be calmed. Someone's got to fix his car. Someone's got to get the blood and gore out of his ride.

When the detective attempts to enter his patrol car the distraught man grabs him by his arm and spins the detective around, "You can't leave me like this!" he shouts. The detective feeling he's being assaulted takes the man to the ground, face first. On goes the cuffs, "You're under arrest!" he says, "You don't put your hands on me!" Into the back seat of the patrol car goes the man. Shock still on his face, he is trying to reason as to why this was happening to him.

At one moment he was driving along, top down, jamming to the beat, breeze blowing through his hair, everything was right with the world. He didn't chop up that guy and place him in his car. He didn't rob anyone. All he was doing was enjoying a sunny day when the death rain poured down on him. Now he's on his way to jail. I guess you could say, when it rains it pours.

The subways, more than what meets the eyes. If only the thousands of people that enter into the belly of this beast could see the visions that are held aside for the chosen few. If only the eyes of the riding public were more open. More open to the sights that would fill them. Like an open barrel left out in a pouring rain an overflow of human mortality would soon blanket them. Even with the great number of lives that it had already claimed, the subway was still hungry for more. The lust for blood could not be quenched.

CHAPTER 14

▼

INFLATION

The next victim to be claimed was a woman. Supthin Blvd. station, rush hour is about to start. A young woman descends the stairway into the dark hole. It would later be learned that she had been released from court only one hour earlier. Arrested for fare evasion the night before, she was given a conviction and released with time served. Handed a subway token after a tongue lashing from the judge, she had regained her freedom.

No one will ever know what the young woman was thinking as she stood on the mezzanine next to the token booth. The clerk on duty paid little or no attention to the woman. She had not approached the booth. She was just waiting for the sound of the train to be heard. This is a safety precaution often practiced by leary persons not wanting to venture deeper into the subway system until they are sure that a train is on its way.

This is also a common sight for someone who doesn't want to pay for the privilege of riding the steel beast. "Not this woman," thought the token clerk, "She doesn't look like a fare beater." Then again what does a fare beater look like? After years of working in the subway the clerk had seen his share of fare beaters and there was no way of telling them apart from a paying passenger. That is until the person had actually paid or not.

As the sound of the approaching train was heard, the woman moved closer to the turnstiles. With one swift move she pulled open the slam gate and ran towards the stairway leading to the southbound platform. With the speed of an

Olympic sprinter she glided down the stairs with her momentum carrying her forward. The train was fast approaching.

There is a man and child sitting on a bench on the platform. They stand in anticipation of the arriving train. Turning their heads in the direction from which the train was coming, they could also see the young woman bounding down the stairs. Her pace is fast. She reaches out with her left hand for the hand-rail, hoping to slow her decent. Her hand slips off of the rail with the speed that she had propelling her forward. The young woman again reached out for the railing in a desperate attempt to stop her decent. Her final grab for the rail is to no avail.

As the train began its entry into the station, the man and child watched helplessly as the young woman sails off the edge of the platform. Slam! The train strikes her. The breaks of the train lock. Sparks flashing from its wheels, the grinding of metal echoes through the station. Not believing what he had just witnessed the man grabs the child, turning him away from the chaos that had unfolded in front of them.

Coming to a jerking halt the train is now still. Out pops the motorman, flashlight in hand. Around the lead car he walks, peering under he spots the figure. Twisted and broken, wedged between the lead car and the second car. Again the scene is the same, only the victim is different. I am the first police officer to arrive at the station.

The smell that hung in the air was unmistakably that of death. Like a thick haze it consumed all breathable air, filling my lungs with its vile odor. Locating the motorman, he takes me over to where the young woman had come to rest. Looking down at her was not an easy thing to do, but it had to be done. The sight of this once living person was hard to take in. Sliced on an angle from her left hip to the right side of her chest, there she was. Face up, eyes open, her life fluids flowing out of the gaping wound. Dead. She was dead under the wheels of a subway car. Why, why did this have to be?

Taking a closer look at the wadded mass, my eyes froze as they came across her right hand. There in the palm was a token, a ninety-cent token. Had she purchased two and did not have the time to place this one in her pocket? Why had the force of the train not dislodged the token from her hand? Who knows why, but there it was, smack in the center of her palm. After interviewing the token clerk, I found out that she had not paid her fare. She had run through the gate in an attempt to keep from having to use her token. The same token that was given to her free from the courthouse, the token that if it had been used could have saved her life.

Instead of having to run full speed for the train, with the use of the token she could have strolled down the stairs. Maybe even had time to sit and talk with the man and child. All this second-guessing is for nothing, for what's done is done. As her body is placed into the back of an ambulance I cannot help but think, "If only she had used that token maybe she would still be alive. But no, there she was wrapped inside of a hefty bag in the back of an ambulance disappearing into the traffic on Hillside Ave. For the remainder of the night my all-consuming thought was, "For a token. For ninety cents she lost her life." The cost of riding the subway had just gone up.

CHAPTER 15

▼

EXPECTATIONS

Life in New York can be hard for anyone, young or old. The real test of a person comes in how he or she deals with what life throws at them. Different people handle stress in different ways. Being a student of the New York City schools can offer its own special challenges. The struggle to fit in with peers for a teenager while also getting good grades can be a soul shredding experience. Wanting to be popular, wanting to be associated with the cool kids. Hanging out, doing what kids do nowadays. Tough thing to do especially when your parents are pushing for you to get good grades, go to college, to follow in the footsteps of your siblings.

The young man we are about to meet had this problem. He knew that his grades were falling. He knew that his family would not accept him doing so poorly. He didn't know how to tell them that he had not passed all of his classes. His grade point average was falling. His teacher had given him a note requesting to talk with his parents. How was he going to face the shame of his family?

Arriving home from school the young man greets his family, no mention of his report card or the note. Glaring at the papers crushed in his hand, the young man sits in his bedroom thinking of how to break the news to his family. His brother and sister had not arrived home yet, for they would be the first to ask about how his schooling was going. He hears his mother talking with someone. It's the neighbor, and she's telling his mother how good her son's report card was.

Stepping out into the living room the young man thinks fast before his mother can ask for his report card. He blurts out, "We need bread, I'm going to the store." His mother stops him in his tracks asking, "Did you get your report card today, can I see it?" The young man states, "I'll show it to you when I get back," and out the door he went.

Walking down Queens Blvd. he comes across one of his buddies, they greet. Telling his friend his problem doesn't help so he walks on. Hours go by, his mother wonders what could be keeping her son so long at the store.

Then it happens, the call, "Man under Grand Ave. northbound side." Here I go again. This scene was no different from the rest. There was the train. The window of the motorman's cab was broken out. That smell again filled the station. This time there weren't any pieces of body that could be recognized as a person. The train had done an efficient job of grinding this young man into something worst than hamburger meat. If not for the clothing and personal papers that they contained, one might have thought that this mess of flesh could have been a stray dog or something, but everyone knew better.

The removal of what remained of the young man didn't take long. In the process of escorting the body bag up to the street, I saw a woman and man running across the mezzanine, the couple was stopped by another officer. They explained how their son had left home to go buy some bread and never returned. The family traced his movements and ran into his friend that he had spoken to.

The friend told them of their son's problem and they were desperately trying to locate him when someone told them about an accident in the subway. Knowing that their son sometimes used the subway as a shortcut across Queens Blvd. they rushed to the station, fearing the worst but hoping for the best. It was not to be. After speaking to the officer, the father and mother were directed over to the detective that was going to be handling the case. They spoke. The detective showed them the papers that were removed from the body, the report card, the teachers note. It's their son.

The mother faints, the father cries. The young man's body is carried past them up to the ambulance. Seems that the young man had lost all hope, he could not face up to his family. At seventeen he felt he was a failure, the black sheep of the family, ending his life was his only way out.

As the motorman recounted his version of what happened he said, "As his train entered the station, the young man came running down the platform towards the approaching train. Faster and faster he ran." Thinking that someone was chasing the young man the motorman reached for his radio to call for the police. Then without notice the young man threw himself into the path of the train, hitting the window of the motorman's cab, bouncing off and falling under the train.

By the time the motorman could stop, all eight cars of the steel beast had passed over the body, each taking its turn slicing, and chopping the young man into the bits that were left. One can only pray for the family that he left behind. It wasn't their fault. They had not thrown their beloved son into the path of that train, or did they? The pressures that a family can put on its members sometimes can be deadly. This was one of those times.

In the last few stories I have tried to give you a look at the darker side of life within the cold concrete walls of the subway. My intention was not to scare, but to enlighten, to inform. If I have done this then you are more aware of your surroundings and my point has been made. If not, well what can I say.

▼

CHAPTER 16

WHEEL OF FORTUNE

It's time to move on, for all of the visions that have flashed before my eyes have not ended in tragedy. There is a softer side to the subway, a side that can also be as funny as hell or just plain stupid. It's all in the eyes of the beholder as to how to interpret the different visions that we are about to experience. I'll be the eyes you are the beholder. You make the call.

Saturday, Woodhaven Blvd, a local station, located above is the Queens Center Mall. Once the mall opens at ten o'clock, the foot traffic is at a feverish pace, shoppers entering, shoppers exiting. Lines of riders waiting to purchase tokens dot the mezzanine. It's bumper-to-bumper people.

Smart riders purchase more then one token in advance. This way when it's time for that return trip home they don't have to wait on those lines. Relaxing next to the token booth, taking a quick coffee break, I'm still alert but seizing a moment to chill. Down the stairway came a young man and woman. They stop to make a phone call. The young man is patting his pockets. Jamming his hand inside he turns them inside out. Something's missing. He asks a question of the young woman, who shakes her head no. As the young man bolts up the stairs the young woman gets in line to buy tokens. Her transaction completed she waits for the young man to come back.

Five minutes, then ten minutes goes by, the young man has not returned. The woman looks at her watch and then glances over to the newspaper stand located inside the turnstiles. She looks back toward the stairway one more time, then places her token in the turnstile and enters. Over to the newsstand she goes, buys a magazine and then heads back over to the row of eight turnstiles to await her partner.

Leafing through the magazine, the minutes go by quickly for the young woman. Trains are breezing past the station. Northbound, southbound, local, express, still she waits. As another train is heard approaching the station, people are scrambling to get through the turnstiles.

Suddenly a voice calls out to the young woman. It's her friend, he yells, "You got them?" She replies, "Yes." The young man bounding across the mezzanine inquires further, "Put it in, put it in, I'm coming, is it in?" "Yes," replies the young woman now standing at the middle turnstile. Her positioning is critical because there is a turnstile on her left and one on her right. There's also the one that she is standing in front of. Into one of the three she has placed a token. The rapidly approaching man has a one in three shot of picking the correct turnstile.

Placing down my coffee I caution the young man to stop running, that he could hurt someone. His reaction was typical of what I had come to expect. "Fuck you," he zinged at me. "You sure it's in," he yells at the young woman. At this time she positions herself in front of the turnstile on her right. Again I shout to the streaking male to stop running. He flashes me the finger, knowing that he will be through the turnstile and on the train before I could ever reach him. Sometimes things don't work out the way you plan.

Boom he hits the turnstile, it doesn't move. Bent in half like a slice of pizza, his legs flew upwards. His upper torso folded over making it look like he was attempting to touch his toes. With the medal bar embedded in his stomach, he let out a painful moan before falling backwards to the floor. Writhing in pain he curled up clutching his midsection. The young woman rushed out to try and render any assistance that she could.

Out comes my radio, "Central, I need an ambulance for a male, injury to his ribs, not a victim of a crime, still conscious." Stepping past the fallen male I reached over and spun the turnstile that held his token. He looks up and states to the young woman, "Why the fuck did you put it in that one, that's not where you were standing!" The young woman just screwed up her face as if saying, "I don't know."

The ambulance arrived in short order. Paperwork was easy, only an aided card to prepare but that wouldn't be doing a complete job. You see the young man as he was being treated was making excuses for how the accident had occurred. With statements like, "I'm going to sue, that fucking turnstile didn't work, I'll sue the city! You saw what happened right officer?" How could I deny that I had not seen it all, of course I had to admit that I had indeed witnessed the entire incident.

There was only one small difference in what I saw and what the young man was stating. But that would all be cleared up when he answered the ticket that I gave him for committing a harmful act. That's right, I gave him a ticket for running in the subway. He had been warned by me not to do so. That he might injure someone. Well, he chose not to listen now he has to pay the price, not once but twice. Ouch, that must hurt.

CHAPTER 17

▼

"CARLOS"

See there are some lighter sides to the subway, as long as the joke is on someone else. Here's one that was on me, you'll like this. Saturday night at the lovely Roosevelt Ave. station, if you want to see it, no matter what it is, you can see it at Roosevelt Ave.

Standing no further than five feet away from the turnstiles making sure everyone can see me. For the end of my tour is creeping up. I'm really ready to leave, to go home and wash the stink of the subway off of me, throw back a beer or two and just relax. No way am I going to take a chance of someone doing something stupid and ruining my plans. I stand out in the open, everyone can see me and I can see them. Again the best-laid plans go astray.

Low and behold some guy hops right over the turnstile. He jumps over right in front of me. Other passengers look to see what my reaction would be. Hell, what else could I do? I stop the guy, who's wearing an ankle length trench coat and requests his ID. He's going to get a ticket at the least. How could he not see me standing there?

In a voice more female than male he states, "I got no ID, I got nothing." Being as stern as possible, I requested the male to search in his pockets again and produce his ID. After turning out the pockets of the coat he repeated in that high-pitched voice, "I got no ID, I got nothing." My response was, "What's under the coat, what's under your coat?" Turning his head to the right the male again says, "I got nothing under my coat." "Open it, open the coat now," I demanded.

Well, I wish that I had never said that because when the coat did open there in front of me stood this naked man. Not one stitch of clothing, his bony frame bare for all to see. "My name is Carlos," he spoke, "Like what you see?" The people watching this unfold burst out laughing.

Any words that I was trying to say froze in my throat before they could reach my lips. What was I to do now? "Close your coat!" I screamed. Looking me up and down while licking his lips this man, want to be woman pipes up in that high-pitched voice, "You told me to open it, I do what you say, you like?" "That's it, you're out of here!" I said. Grabbing the male while holding his coat close at the same time, I assisted him up the stairs to the street. "Now go away!" I stated, "And don't come back." "You so strong, I like it rough," is what I heard as I slink back into the hole.

As I arrived back on the mezzanine the people that had watched the action gave me an ovation, clapping their hands and still laughing. One woman walks over to me and states, "You must love your job, you get to meet such nice people, God bless you!" The sight of Carlos naked, his little Vienna Sausage dangling, head propped over to the right and his words, made me laugh also for the remainder of the night. I swear you cannot make this stuff up.

CHAPTER 18

▼

HEADS UP

There came a night I found myself fixed at 169th street station the entire tour. Another eight hours on one station. Walking back and forth one end to another, nothing happening. This was going to be a long night. It's the middle of winter, snow coming down in blankets. Covering the city in its white foam, no one is out. The streets are bare. The token clerk and myself are the two lone inhabitants of this lonely hole. How am I going to make eight hours out here? A thought came to me. Maybe if I watched the turnstiles long enough someone would beat the fare. Maybe there is another person out in this snowy mess of a night. What else did I have to do? I'll give it a shot.

Taking up a position halfway down the stairs leading to the southbound platform I stood back against the wall, hat off just waiting, hoping that someone would step into my trap. The time passed by slowly, minutes seemed to be hours. I waited and waited, eyes fixed on the turnstiles, shuffling from left foot to right foot. Someone must be out. The whole city can't be sitting at home watching television.

The trains come, the trains go, people get off, but no one enters the station. Lord help me, just one person that's all I need. Just one person to come down and not pay, maybe even a smoker, a person urinating, anything that's against the laws of the subway, a person to take my mind off of the loneliness. I could talk to the clerk but he's sleeping. Now that's an easy job for a night like this. You know,

I might not even issue a ticket for a violation. I'm at the point where any human contact would be a nice change of pace.

When I had just about given up, low and behold I observed a male peeking around the corner from the street stairway. Yeah come on, take a good look around, he can't see me, but I can see him. The man walks toward the token booth, doesn't buy a token. This looks like a potential ticket situation, a break in the humdrum. Lying in wait, I watch as the man stands in front of the turnstiles, head moving from left to right, eyes searching for any sign of a cop.

He retrieves a beer from his coat pocket, takes a sip, then he lights a cigarette. Feeling good about himself he begins to sing. Whatever his day job is he should not give it up. I've heard dogs barking that sounded better than him. Drinking, smoking and singing his heart out he waits. Me too. After finishing his beer and cigarette he walks over to the street stairway.

My mind is telling me he's gonna leave, but no he places the now empty can down and takes up a leaning position on the handrail. A northbound train is approaching, he listens noting which direction the train is going. It's not the one he wants. As the train unloads its passengers, I watch as the people make their way up and out. Back to my subject of attention, where is he? He's gone. He must have been waiting for someone that got off that train. I guess I was wrong, that guy wasn't up to anything. I must have been over zealous in my wanting.

So here I am, still on the stairway, alone again. A southbound train is approaching the station. I put my hat on, got to look professional for my public. As the train enters the station I take one final look at the turnstile area nothing, no one. Giving up on my search I headed up the stairs, when all of a sudden here he comes. The same guy, running full speed heading in the direction of the turnstiles, he didn't leave, he was waiting upstairs.

Now taking a closer look I can see that he has another beer in his hand, he went to get a beer. With his mind set on making his train he doesn't even see me standing at the top of the stairs. He's going for the gate I think, I'm ready, lets get this show on the road. Not breaking stride he sprints forward. No, he's not going for the gate he's heading for the turnstiles he's going to jump over.

If he does that and hits the ground running it's going to be hard to catch up with him. Getting myself ready to chase after him I remove my hat and take out my stick, I'm ready. I watch as the man without breaking stride takes a flying leap, airborne he sails over the turnstiles, but there is a problem.

For all his effort and grace, he didn't quite get it right. Hanging above the turnstiles was a thick metal sign that showed which trains stopped at this station. As the man soared through the air he didn't keep his head tucked. Bam! He crashed into the sign, losing his balance he falls backwards. Thud! He hits the ground. Sprawled out on the mezzanine he rolls around in pain.

I head over to him, he's dazed, unable to stand, and a knot the size of an apple is protruding from his forehead. Asking, "Are you alright," I attempt to assess his condition. Holding back my laughter I stare down at him. With his eyes still closed he mumbles, "Get the fuck away from me, leave me alone." Now I see blood coming from the back of his head I say, "Guy I'm going to call you an ambulance, ok." "Fuck you and your ambulance I don't need your help."

Gaining his senses he gets to his feet, he touches the knot on his forehead, then reaches around to the back and winches in pain. Seeing the blood from the back of his head he then ties a bandana around his head. He proceeds over to the token booth, buys a token and walks back over to the turnstiles. I inquire one more time, asking, "Are you sure you're alright?" Giving me the fickle finger he drops his token into the turnstile and walks through.

With one final look back at me he asked, "When the hell did they put that there? I didn't see that fucking sign. Everyday I jump this turnstile. That shit wasn't there before. They put that shit up there just for me, huh? Just to bust my head. Fuck you."

After the male left, the clerk called me over to the booth. He said that the sign had been placed up there that morning but they were coming back tomorrow to fix it because it was to low. "Well it served its purpose tonight," I said, "Taught that guy a lesson."

The rest of the night went by without any other situations arising. No tickets, no people. I boarded the train back to my command. Halfway back to the command I heard my radio, listening I heard as the operator put out the job, "Any unit 169th street, we have a report of a male tearing down a sign on the mezzanine, male is armed with a hammer." I think to myself he's back, he's getting revenge on that sign. Central added further, "Units be advised the male also has a knot on his forehead. Any unit to check and advise."

The patrol car is enroute. I continue on to the command. After getting dressed in my street clothes, I am about to leave the command when in walks the guy in handcuffs, knot on forehead, bandana still wrapped around the cut. He looked at me and stated, "I won't hit my head on that shit again.

CHAPTER 19

▼

A STICKY SITUATION

Sometimes after seeing some of the things that people do in the subways I wonder, what could they have been thinking, why would anyone do such a thing? Case in point, one of the strangest things that I have ever seen happened at the 179th street station.

I watched as men went in and out of the restrooms. In the subway you gotta keep a keen eye on any open restrooms, almost anything goes on inside of them. An elderly man entered. As time goes on I didn't notice if he came out or not. After fifteen minutes I go to give a check. Before reaching the restroom, a young man stops me and says, "You better check on that old guy in there, something's wrong with him."

Into the restroom I go, there's the old-timer sitting on the bowl. "You alright, I asked. "I can't get up," he replies. "What you mean you can't get up, you sick or something, what's wrong?" "I can't get up I told you, my ass is stuck to the seat," he growls. "Yeah right pops. Get your butt up and get out of here," is my response, "You got ten seconds." Shaking his fist at me he says, "If I could I would. If you don't believe me you get me up."

On goes the gloves, I take the man by his arm and try to lift him, he doesn't move. I can't budge him. He's stuck tight to the seat. With each tug he rises just a bit, but the seat also rises with him. I'm stumped, what is going on here? I tell the old-timer to sit tight I'll be right back.

Putting something like this over the radio, I wouldn't know what to say. So over to the phone I go. After telling the desk officer what my problem was he says, "Good joke guy, now get back to work." He didn't believe me. No choice, I gotta use the radio. "Central send me Emergency Rescue, I have a man stuck to the toilet seat." The radio operator is cracking up. "What was that unit?" I repeated my message. This time Central replies, "10/4 unit standby."

The rescue unit and any cop in the area show up. Everyone is looking at the old guy on the toilet. He pipes up, "I'm not a freak show, what the hell you all looking at!" It took sometime but finally the old guy was released from the toilet. Released from the toilet but not the seat. It had been removed from the bowl but not from the man's rear. Wrapped in a blanket the old-timer was lead up to an ambulance. Face down he was placed onto a stretcher, seat still gripping his rear.

The medic steps out of the ambulance and states, "He's glued to the seat. Somehow he got glued to the seat. We got to take him in. I don't know how they're going to get it off. You coming with us?" I wanted to go but I've seen enough. "No you take him, but first let me ask him a question." "Hey guy how did this happen?" He didn't know. All he knew was that he had to use the toilet really bad. When he went inside there was some other guy just sitting on the bowl with his pants on not using it, so he demanded that the guy get up.

After cursing at the old-timer the guy got up but hesitated for a second. The old-timer in his rush to relieve himself did not inspect the bowl before taking his seat. Turns out that for reasons only known to the other man, before he left the toilet he had spread super glue on the seat.

A few days had gone by and I was back at 179th street, over to me comes the old-timer. "Remember me," he asked. "Yeah, how could I forget you," I say, "How's it going? How did you make out with that problem you had?" Shaking his head he tells me that at the hospital they had to remove the skin from his rear in order to free him from the seat. "I gotta shit standing up now," he said "You ever tried to shit standing up, why would anyone do this to me? That's alright though, I know what that motherfucker looks like. When I see him again, I'm gonna put my foot up his ass and see how he likes it." With that he turned and started to walk away. I couldn't help but notice that he walked with a hitch in his step. Gently easing himself along. I thought to myself, "Damn they skinned his ass, that gotta hurt."

CHAPTER 20

▼

A. CLEAN UP WOMAN

If you have ever traveled on the subway, I'm pretty sure that at some point in time you have come across a panhandler, someone begging for money. In my job I saw them everyday, each with their own sad sob story. The beggar enters a subway car filled with people, each involved in their own world. The people try to ignore the beggar, keeping their heads down, hoping not to make eye contact. Just let him or her move past me they hope. Some reach into their pockets and fork over money, a penny, a dime, the big score a dollar.

In the past I tried to warn the riding public not to give money to those people. But all I would get back was something like, "If it was you, you would want us to give you money. How can you deny those people? They aren't robbing anyone, they aren't stealing, leave them alone."

What most of the kind-hearted passengers didn't know or chose to ignore was that the stories that were being spun by the destruct beggars were not true. I don't mean to say that every beggar I've come across who had a sob story was lying. No, some of them were for real but ninety five percent of them are just lies to get easy money. Remember I had tried to warn the passengers.

One day while doing some plainclothes work, my partner and I watched as a young woman entered the train car we were sitting in. Fitting in well with the regular passengers she paid no attention to us. She proceeds to spin her tale of down fall. How she had lost everything. She was trying to feed her children. Trying to put clothes on their backs. She was telling how bad the shelters in the city were. How she was trying to get herself and her kids out. "Please, anything you can spear would be of a great help."

I watched as people dug deep into their pockets or purses and forked over money to this woman. She made a killing. I mean the train had ten cars and if you added up what she was given from each car, she was raking in the dough.

My partner and I followed this woman as she left the train at the 74th street station. What was she going to do now buy drugs, buy some liquor? No not this woman. We followed her out of the station into the streets of Roosevelt Ave. She stops on the corner of 75th Ave. and Broadway. We watch from across the street. "What's she up to?" we wonder.

That question would be answered in the form of a Mercedes. Yes, a Mercedes, the car that most people crave but are not able to buy. A car that makes some people drool or stare at in awe as it rolls by.

The Mercedes pulls up to the curve and a young man pops out the driver's side. The young woman walks over to him, gives him a kiss and hug. My partner and I exchange looks of disbelief. The young man asks, "How was your day, get a good take?" Opening her shopping bag she replies, "You tell me." The young man now aglow, hugs the young woman again while saying, "That's my girl."

After placing her bag in the trunk of the car, the woman takes out a three quarter length fur coat and hands it to her friend. She then removes the dirty jeans and sweater she was wearing. Under them are black leather pants and a silk blouse. She throws her work clothes into the trunk then slams it shut. She puts on her fur and has a seat behind the wheel of the car. The two sit there for a moment. My partner and I make our way closer to the car. The two are laughing and joking with each other.

Before they drove away my partner and myself overheard the male saying, "Look I need to borrow the car tomorrow, is it ok with you?" The young woman spat back at him, "I work hard to get what I got, you need to get off your ass and get a job." With that said they drove off into the night.

Six weeks later the young woman was arrested for scamming the public. Upon her arrest her statement to me was, "How much do you make? I could buy and sell your ass! I'll be out tomorrow and I'll be back on the subway too, so fuck you."

The very next day while on my way to work, I was reading the paper when all of a sudden I heard that voice. It was her. Looking up we made eye contact. Off the train she ran. As the doors closed and the train began to move, through the window I saw her. Giving me the finger and shouting," Fuck you, I told you I'll be back," she barked at me.

This woman was arrested numerous times but she kept coming back to the subways. Why, because that's where the money is. That's her job, to get the money.

▼

CHAPTER 21

BREW...HA...HA...

The subway can be the perfect place to obtain what you are looking for, if your goals are set low enough that is. Take for example the day I came across a guy begging for money on the mezzanine of the 71st. Ave. station. This guy was not your typical beggar. He wasn't telling a tall tale of bad luck. He wasn't making any wild claims. No, he was just stating his needs. He needed to buy a drink.

Calling out to the people that passed his way he spoke the words, "I'm not going to lie to you. I'm a drunk and I'm asking anyone to be so kind as to help me out in getting my next drink." He stood out of the path of the traveling public not obstructing them in anyway. The spot that he had chosen was ideal. He wasn't getting in the way but he was visible enough for everyone to see.

As his call for assistance went in and out of the ears of the non-sympathetic passengers he changed his tune to that of a song that everyone knew. With the tunes of one hundred bottles of beer on the wall he put on a one man show. Singing and dancing he was now the figure of attention for everyone. With his hat lying on the ground in front of him, he would insert his cry for help in buying another drink, "Eighty cans of beer on the wall, eighty cans of beer, all of those cans of beer on the wall and I got none at all, a can, a quart, a forty ounce and out I will bounce."

The group of people that had gathered to enjoy the show laughed. Some even gave him money. As I made my way over to the entertaining male he seemed to quicken his pace. The words came out faster. His jumping about became more frantic. Ending his one-man show before I could get to him, I watched as he retrieved his hat containing his spoils and up the stairs he flew.

A few hours zipped by as the night crept on. Taking a stroll down the platform on my way to the part time side, I happened to spot the same guy sitting on a bench. For some reason he didn't look happy. "What's the problem," I asked. "All that time I wasted making my money and some kid snatches my hat. I'm still dry, gotta try and make more."

Looking into his blood shot eyes I could tell that he was really suffering from his lost. Unable to satisfy his craving for booze he was deep in thought as to what to do next. "You want to make a report?" I asked. "What the hell's that gonna do," he zinged my way. "Is making a report gonna get me my drink?" With that said I moved on.

At the rear of the station is where the cleaner heaps the garbage that he has collected during the day. "Who's that over there?" I wonder. There's someone picking through the bags of garbage. It's not the cleaner. It's some bum and he's making a mess. Heading towards this person I realize it's the drunk

He spots me and heads back down towards the bench. I go over to him. "What were you doing in the garbage?" I asked. Looking up at me he pipes, "People throw out some good shit. I was just checking. I didn't do anything wrong." Showing me a large can of beer, he continues, "See I found this, almost a full can. It's not my brand but who cares." "Give me that," I say, "You can't drink that down here." "Who's gonna stop me, you?" he asked.

Lifting the can to his mouth he took a large chug, enjoying every drop of the sweet mix. After gulping it down, his mouth became full and suddenly he began to spit. Cursing and spitting he throws the can down. "What's your problem?" I asked. Thinking he has gotten upset and maybe he's ready to fight.

Still spitting he jumps to his feet, wiping his mouth with the sleeve of his shirt. He turns in my direction and with the look of disgust on his face he yells out, "That's not beer, that's piss! I just drank piss!" Holding back my chuckles I instructed him to pick up the can and throw it in the garbage.

No problem, over to the can he goes, picks it up and then to the garbage he shuffles. Lifting the lid he drops the can in. Then he spots another bottle, out comes his newest find. After what just happened to him I know he's not going to drink this stuff. Well, I was wrong. Smiling he takes a gulp. I'm thinking well he got lucky, he found a good one. Wrong, again he began to spit and curse. Yelling at the top of his lungs he spouts, "Why the fuck are all these cans filled with piss, what the fuck is going on?" When his tirade is over he apologizes to me for making a scene. After that he leaves the station with his head hung low.

If he had stuck around I could have answered his question. The reason that there were so many cans filled with piss was that the toilets were closed. After drinking a can or two of beer when you gotta go, you gotta go. So why not refill the can. Too bad for him he didn't take the time to inspect his finds more closely, that would have saved him a mouthful of piss.

CHAPTER 22

▼

HAPPY MOTHER'S
DAY

The visions that I am writing about could only be seen in the subways. No place else had I come across such things. The sight of people's faces as they endured the bad luck that had befallen them was priceless. Whatever makes a person do the things that seem to come to them naturally in the subway is beyond me. All I know is that observing the outcome of the different situations made for a very entertaining day.

It's Mother's day. I'm at Grand Ave. again the day is moving along at a good pace. Watching all the women dressed in their best. Proudly displaying to the world, yes I am a mother. Every one of the women that I see is dressed to kill. Some are going out for dinner. Others are going over to relatives to spend the day. Wherever they are going they look good and they know it. Taking in the sights of all the well-groomed women I start to make a game out of it. Who's gonna get the prize for the best dressed mother of the day.

At the far end of the station there is a tall high-wheel that will permit passengers to exit but not enter. Quite a few passengers take advantage of this. Instead of walking all the way down to the turnstiles they could just push through the wheel and quickly exit the station. I guess someone else thought about the easy exit also but not in the usual way.

Still watching as the parade of mothers went on, I started noticing that every once in a while when someone would exit out the high-wheel that they would stop and stare at their hands. Then proceed to wipe them off with tissue or whatever was handy. About five or six people had done this, so I decided to go take a look at the high-wheel. Maybe there's some oil on it. Maybe it needs to be cleaned. I didn't think that anyone was getting injured because no one had approached me complaining of being hurt.

Before I reached the high-wheel a couple had exited. They stopped and stared at their hands, then looked at the high wheel. The husband could be heard cursing and wondering out loud, "Why?" "How you doing," I say, "Is everything alright?" "No!" the woman says. "Look at our hands," holding out their palms to show me. I observe something caked on their fingers. "What's that?" I say. "It's shit. Someone put shit on the wheels. Look at what they did."

Shining my flashlight on the metal hand bars I could see that about waist high on every other bar there was indeed some sort of substance. Upon closer examination, the sniff test that is, I realized that this was shit. The shit was placed in such a way that anyone exiting out through the wheel would have to place their hands directly in it.

Offering my apologies to the couple I escort them to the restroom so that they could clean up. The husband is still fuming, "Look at her dress," he says, "There's shit all over it. How we gonna go eat with her dress covered in shit?" Not knowing what to say, I said nothing. "I just bought this yesterday, look at it. It's ruined," the woman began to cry.

Her husband holds her in his arms trying his best to comfort her. He strokes her hair. He rubs her back. Then without hesitation the woman pushes away. "You smell like shit." she says, "Let me see your sleeve." Holding out his arms he asks, "What, you see something on my shirt?" By pointing not wanting to touch, she directs him to look on the underside of his sleeve. There it was a long line of shit going from cuff to the elbow. The woman spins around, "Check my back," she says. There on her shoulder and mid back was another line of the foul stuff.

When her husband had caressed her he smeared her with what was on his shirt. I'm thinking this is a sad sight here. These people got all dressed up to go out and have a good time. Dressed in their best. Now look at them, covered in shit. After cleaning up the best they could in the restroom the couple decided the best thing to do was to go back home. I stayed with them on the platform trying my best to reassure the shitty couple. I didn't want to tell them that the smell that was coming from them was bad, so I didn't.

The train finally arrives and we say our goodbyes. I watch as the couple enters. As the doors close I could see the other passengers moving away from the couple, some shaking their heads, some holding their noses. They were going to have a whole section of that train car to themselves. Why would someone put shit on the high-wheel, for what? There wasn't anyone watching to see the reactions of the unlucky ones that came into contract with it, so why do it? People do the damndest things in the subway.

CHAPTER 23

▼

HEATED UP

Now I don't want to give you the impression that only the public did stupid or outrageous things in the subway. The cops and the transit employees also had their moments. Let's start with one of the cops. Friday, it's a hot sweltering day in the city. The temperature hit ninety-eight degrees. It's hot and sticky. Even the slightest movement brings beads of moisture to the skin. While getting dressed for patrol, I noticed another officer also getting suited up for the day. This was nothing out of the ordinary because I shared the row of lockers with fifteen others.

There was however something odd about this officer though. He was red as a lobster. Each movement he made brought the unmistaken look of pain to his face. Observing the amount of pain he was suffering, I had to ask, "What happened to you, why you so red?" "I fell asleep in my backyard while trying to get a tan, guess I over did it." That was an understatement. Over did it. No, over done is more like it, well cooked.

Assisting the officer on with his vest I thought, he's not going to make it tonight. He might as well have called out sick. Strapping on his vest was a chore in itself, with every pull of the straps he moaned in pain. I'm like, "Guy you ain't gonna make it out the door, look at you." Half bent over in agony he barks out, "Just help me on with my belt, I'll do the rest." On goes the belt. Watching him buckling it almost brought tears to my eyes. This poor guy is about to pass out. "Guy you gotta go home. There's no way you're gonna make it through the tour." "Look, I'm chronic sick already. I don't have the personal time to take off. What the hell am I supposed to do? I'll make it, alright."

Roll call comes and goes, he got through that. Out the door we go, headed for different parts of the city. I'm going north, he's going south. I wish him well. The tour goes by without a hitch, no problems and no hassles. This is amazing for New York on such a hot day, not one problem all tour. Aha, yes it's time to be heading back to the command. Time to get the hell out of this uniform and go home. Just removing the vest would give me such joy. Not to mention being able to suck up some air conditioning to cool down my smoldering body. My uniform was sticking to me in places I didn't even know I had. It had to come off.

As I reached the doors of the command I could see the rest of my platoon milling around outside the doors. Why isn't anyone going inside? What's up? Out pops the Sergeant. He's looking for the sun burnt officer. He inquires to each officer outside the door whether or not they had seen the sun burnt officer. Everyone answers no not since roll call. Here we are five feet from the refreshing air that blew inside of the command. Five feet away from ripping off the uniforms and letting our bodies breathe, five feet away from being released from our sweaty prisons.

"Alright guys," the Sergeant starts, "Until we find the officer no one leaves, so fall in for a head count." "No, no he didn't say that. It's time to go, this is my time. I can't take this heat any longer. I gotta get out of here," is what runs through my mind. "Why do we have to stand out here?" I say, "Why not do this inside? I'm hot. We're all hot and by us standing out here ain't gonna make the cop you're looking for appear."

The glare that was sent my way by the Sergeant said it all. He was hot also. He wanted to go home too. But no, he's stuck here like us until the cop is found. "Listen up guys," is what came from his mouth, "Until we find this officer no one leaves. No one. We are not the only people being held over. Any cop that worked our tour in the city is being held. No one leaves until he's found."

Now I know it made sense to hold over my commands tour, but the entire city. That's thousands of cops being held over. That's millions of dollars being paid out by the city in overtime. Did I say overtime? Hey, this might not be too bad after all. I'm hot, I'm still sweating but I'm not doing anything and not being asked to do anything but standby. Standby and get paid time and a half, I can do that. All of a sudden it's not that hot anymore. Look don't get me wrong, I'm not that cold hearted that I can forget about a missing officer, but there's no talk of him being in any danger or something. There are no reports of an officer down any place.

I listen as the radio broadcasts the name and shield number of the missing officer. Over and over the broadcast is placed. The entire police department of this great city is either mobilized to find him or on lock down. Hours pass, the whereabouts of the officer is unknown. I'm still standing in front of the command with the rest of my sweaty group. This has gone on too long. Making overtime was fine at the start but now who needs it. The whole atmosphere has changed. I'm really worried about this cop. At first I was thinking he would show up in a few minutes, maybe his radio went dead or maybe he missed his train.

Those thoughts went down the drain as the hours went by. Even if his radio were dead, if he had missed his train to return, he would have called by now. He must be hurt. Lord he might even be dead. As all kinds of awful visions flashed in my mind, as the hours grew longer I started to lose hope of seeing this cop again.

Maybe I should have said something about his condition. How much pain he was in, how bad he looked in the locker room. Maybe I should have but I didn't and I wasn't about to say anything now. Opening my mouth now would bring down the wrath of every cop standing in the roasting subway with me.

Where could he be? He couldn't just disappear. How could a cop in full uniform fall off the face of the earth? Where the hell is he? The stress is getting to everyone no one is saying a word. All ears are listening to the radio. Over and over his description is put out over the airways.

In all the silence the sound of keys jingling is heard coming down the passageway leading to the command. All heads turn to see who it is. Clearing the passage we see it's him. It's the cop the whole city is looking for. He's alright. He's not dead and he's not hurt. The platoon rushes over to greet him. He laughs and states, "What's up? Why you guys still here? What's going on?"

The relief that was felt by everyone had past as quickly as it came. Now we're mad. "Where the hell have you been? Do you know the whole city is looking for you?" the Sergeant was cutting into him like a hot knife through butter. "Central, be advised we found the officer. Repeat we found the officer. He's alright, he's at the command, you can release the troops now. I'll call you with details via phone."

Grabbing the dazed cop by his arm the Sergeant repeats, "Where the fuck were you, all these guys are stuck here because you're missing? Where the fuck were you!!" No one, not one officer moved. Yeah, we wanted to go home but this guy was gonna tell us something first.

Looking around at the angry group he started, "I fell asleep. I went into a room to take a break the next thing I knew it was three o'clock in the morning." Rubbing his head and clinching his fist the Sergeant barked, "Why didn't you call? Why didn't you answer your radio? What are you brain dead? His answer was as stupid as he seemed to be, "I thought I would be able to slip in and slip out without anyone noticing me. If I answered the radio I would have given myself up. My bad, I'm sorry."

The looks that were given to this officer as we filed past him would have stopped a charging bull in his tracks, but to the burnt sleepy officer they had no effect. After his return from his suspension he was given a new nickname that he carried with him for the rest of his career. That name was, "Sleepy." This is only one example of cops acting stupid.

CHAPTER 24

▼

BOOGIE NIGHT

Here's another one. Somehow summer brings out the partying mood in people. Maybe it's the hot steamy days and nights. Or maybe it's the natural instincts after observing half dressed people most of the day.

Being young and a cop can also cause all sorts of problems. The longing to go out with your friends and boogie down has to be set aside because the job comes first. There you are on your way to work while your buddies are gearing up for a night out on the town. You'll soon be gearing up for a night in the subway. What a tradeoff this is.

Here you are on a Friday or Saturday night putting on the blues, while your friends are out shaking their butts on a dance floor. Well you knew this before you took the job, there were going to be sacrifices that had to be made. Some of the younger officers had come to realize this, some of them didn't. For the ones that couldn't get it straight there was going to be a hefty price to pay. Work, party, which was more important? Which would lead to a better life, a better you? Decisions had to be made. Making the wrong one was easy to do.

We're back to that Saturday night. A female officer eight months out of the academy is getting dressed for her tour. She tells another female officer how her boyfriend wanted to take her to a house party that night. She also tells how she had called and requested an excusal, but was denied by some fatheaded Sergeant. How she wished that she could be dancing the night away instead of having to do the northbound southbound boogie in the subway. What a waste of a Saturday.

What a waste of her youth. Having put aside her partying days for six months while attending the academy and for another eight months while out on the road learning the ropes, she was itching to get back into the swinging life.

Before she leaves the command for her assignment, she decides to give one more shot at getting off. Over to the desk she glides. Batting her eyes at the desk officer while attempting to put forward her, hey there big fellow look. She starts by saying, "You look different, have you been working out?" Flashing back a look of what's she up to, the desk officer accepts the compliment. He turns his head back to his paperwork trying to ignore the female officer standing in front of him.

After a few seconds goes by and the officer is still standing at the desk, the Sergeant feeling that she had something else on her mind inquires, "Is there something I can help you with? Do you have a problem?" Building up her nerves the young female officer in her most sultry voice states, "Seems like there are a lot of officers working tonight. Every post is covered, all the cars are filled." "Yeah, it's a full house," the Sergeant replies. "Well anyway since you got all these officers working tonight I thought that maybe I could be excused. I mean it's not like you'll miss me. See I got invited to a party and when I called up earlier and asked to be excused I was told no. So now that I see how many people are working tonight I thought maybe you'll let me go, ok."

Leaning on the desk with her chin in her palm she waited. Eyes fluttering, passing her tongue over her lips she waited for an answer. Without even lifting his eyes from the papers he was reviewing the Sergeant gives her the answer she didn't want to hear, "You were told no once and you're being told no again, so get to post!"

Out the door she goes. Under her breath she's calling the Sergeant every bad word she can think of. On her way to post all she can think about is how she could be dancing, drinking and having a good time instead of standing in the subway watching the rats go by and smelling the scent of human urine all night.

For two hours she thought of a way to get out of the subway. With each thought came a curse for the Sergeant and for the job. How could they do this to her? Then an idea popped into her partying mind. The only Sergeant working tonight was sitting in the command at the desk. There was not going to be anyone looking for her. All she had to do was make rings via the phone every two hours to the command to let them know everything was alright.

Over to the pay phone she dashed. Dialing her boyfriend, listening to the ringing of the phone, "Pick up, answer the damn phone," she said to herself. "Hello," Thank God he answered. Without taking a breath she proceeded to lay out her plan to her boyfriend. "You still at home?" she asked. "Yeah," he says.

"Good, pick me out a nice outfit and shoes, put them in the car and meet me at my station. I'll change in the car while you drive." "What you talking about?" Her boyfriend states, "Don't you gotta work?" Wondering how she's planning to pull this off. "Shut up and listen," she shouts into the phone, "Just do what I say, I'll be waiting." "Ok, ok, I'll be there in a little bit," he responds.

Searching through her closet he picks out the skimpiest outfit he can find. She'll look great in this he thinks. After placing her clothing into the car, he zips off to retrieve his girl. At the station she waits perfecting her master plan for the night. The boyfriend pulls up. She hops into the passenger seat, "go, go," she says. Driving away from the station the boyfriend watches as the young female officer changes from her uniform into her party clothes. "How you gonna get away with this," he asked while taking in the sight of his half dressed companion.

Without missing a beat she tells him of her plan. "They won't miss me," she says, "There's no Sergeant on the road tonight. All I gotta do is call in every once in a while to let them know I'm ok. Then you get me back to the command by my time to get off and no one will know. Got me. Know what I'm saying?" Her plan sounded good to him, so onto the party they went.

With the music pumping and the drinks flowing they were having a good old time. A check of her watch told her it was time to call the command. She rushes out the door and into the car. Then she pulls out her cell and calls in, "What's up it's me," she says, "I'm making a ring in, everything is fine." Holding her breath she waits for a response. "Ok got'cha, stay safe," the Sergeant says, "Sorry about that excusal thing but our excusal list was filled up for tonight, maybe next time. Watch your back out there." Hanging up the phone she laughs, "If he only knew." Back to the party she goes.

Oh what a night. She had not enjoyed herself like this in over a year and it showed. Not missing a dance, not passing on any drinks she turned the party out. Noticing that his girl was getting out of control the boyfriend decided to put an end to the night. "Look, it's about time we get out of here. I gotta take you back, you ready?"

Taking her by the arm they headed to the car. "Get dressed," he stated to her. All the drinking had taken its toll on the young officer. She struggled to get out of her party clothes and back into her uniform. With her mind spinning she lost all track of what she was doing. "Look you gotta focus," the boyfriend says, "Hurry up and get dressed."

The car stops at a red light up beside it comes a city bus. Inside the car the young female is still trying to make the clothing switch. From the bus is heard the shouts of some young men who had spotted the half-dressed woman in the car.

"Yo baby take it all off. Let's see what you got." The whistling and catcalling kept coming, as the young men were getting an eye full of her body. Not wanting to risk being pulled over, the boyfriend didn't want to run the light. They had to sit there and take it. "You gonna let them talk that way to me?" the young woman barked at her boyfriend. Holding back on his emotions he tried to calm her down. "What the hell you want me to do? You ain't supposed to be here. We can't get into any trouble. I gotta get you back!"

The night of drinking had hit the young officer hard. She had no control over her thoughts. The liquor had taken over. "Well if you ain't gonna do something I will," she shouted. Still nude from the waist up she leans out the window of the car. Gun in hand she yells, "Fuck you motherfuckers!" The guys on the bus who were catcalling at this now armed beauty ducked for cover.

Bang! Bang! Bang! The shots rang out. "I'll kill you, you bitches!" she yells while still pulling the trigger. Bang! Bang! Another volley of shots rang out. The boyfriend not believing what is happening, steps on the gas. Away they fly. "What the fuck you doing!" he screams. "That'll show them you don't fuck with me!" the young woman shouts. The rest of the drive is silent. Thinking how lucky they were, the boyfriend pulls up to her station. "Get out, I'll call you later," he says.

Out the car and into the subway the young officer goes. Stumbling but trying to be cool she makes her way to the platform. Gotta make it back to the command. Gotta get back on time she thinks. As she leans on the door of the train passengers start to stare. The smell of booze coming off of the officer is strong. They watch as she struggles to maintain her balance. What a sight. The train pulls into the home station of the command. She made it. Up the stairs she goes trying her best to look and act normal.

Gotta get some gum she thinks. To the candy stand she goes. "Give me a pack of Big Red," she says. The guy behind the counter asks, "You alright officer?" "Just give me the gum," she says. With his eyes in disbelief the counter guy hands over the gum. "You better go sleep it off," he says. "Fuck you!" she growls. Chewing hard on the gum the officer heads into the command. "Don't talk to anyone, go straight to your locker, change and get out," she thinks to herself.

Opening the door to the command she sees a wall of blue. There's so many gold shields around it looks like Fort Knox. "There she is," the Sergeant says, "Come here. What the hell you been doing? Where the hell have you been?" Before she could come up with a lie, she notices a city bus driver standing in the corner. "That's her. That's the one. She shot up my bus."

With that said the young officer was taken into the Captain's office where she came face to face with the young men that were on the bus. The same young men that she had tried to kill while in her drunken rage. "That bitch is crazy," one of the young men said, "Crazy but fine. Damn she's fine." "Yo baby, do me and I'll forget the hold thing," one of the guys says. "Do you! Shit that bitch tried to do us all," the bus driver says. Busted. How did they find out who she was she wondered. They had sped away right after she shot. The street was dark how did they know who she was?

That question was answered fast enough. When the car ran the red light to get away, the fleeing couple had not noticed that there was a foot cop standing on the corner. He didn't have the chance to fire at the car but he did get the plate number. The car was registered to her so with a check of the system wham, got'cha. Her boyfriend was brought into the command a short time later. The two were arrested and charged with attempted murder. A career and two lives shot to hell, all for wanting to party. Again, I must say, you cannot make this stuff up.

CHAPTER 25

▼

IT'S MY PARTY

The desire for wanting to hang out is not only for the female officers. Far from it, male officers also have the craving. Take for example a young male officer. He had been on the job for three years. In those three years he had never been able to attend his own birthday party. For some reason he was always denied an excusal, why I don't know. Could it have been the way he carried himself? The way he talked to others? His personality? Still I don't know. But what I do know is that for some reason he rubbed a lot of people the wrong way.

Whenever he spoke it was like he was talking down to you. When dealing with the public he always had problems. Belittling anyone that he would have to make contact with. He was rude, obnoxious, and cross. If someone were to ask him for simple directions or how to get somewhere his usual response would be, "You left home and don't know where you're going? That's dumb. How can you be going some place and not know how to get there?"

Most of the time the person seeking the directions would just ignore his smart remarks. Some would walk away. Others would fire back with something like, "It's your job to know how to get around the city that's why I'm asking you. If you don't know just say so." This type of response would only lead to more verbal abuse from the overconfident officer. "I'm not the one lost. I know where I'm at and where I'm going, you're the one that's lost." As if talking to a five-year-old he would go through the directions adding in a little snide remark here and there.

This officer had a gift for getting under your skin. Perhaps that's why he was denied his birthday off. I mean who would be throwing him a party? Who could stand to associate with him when they did not have to? I could only think of two people, his mother and his father. That is if they even liked him.

Well here it is his big day, the day that this crass person was brought into this world. Before roll call he is on the telephone. I overhear him say, "I got it all planned, just be there at seven. I got everything set." Whatever it was he had planned brought a big smile to his face. Roll call starts. He's still on the phone. Calling out his name the Sergeant gets no response. He calls for him again, still no answer. "Has anyone seen officer so and so?" the Sergeant asks. "Yeah he's on the phone," a voice says. "Could someone please tell Mr. Popular that his presence is requested at roll call?"

Strolling into the muster room not a care in the world, the birthday boy has a seat and acts as if the Sergeant is disturbing him. His name is called out one more time. He answers and his assignment is read out. It's not the one he thought he had. "Why was I changed, why don't I have what was posted last night?" he fumes.

Without coming across as putting the screws to him the Sergeant replies, "Maybe if you were here on time you wouldn't have been changed." Glaring at the Sergeant with a look of hate the officer demands, "I'm here now and I want my assignment back. You had no right to change me. I was here on time and I'm here now. That's my assignment and I'm going to keep it!"

All heads turn to the Sergeant, what's he gonna say? How is he going to handle this loud mouth? With the cool of a professional the Sergeant calmly states, "I'm in charge here and you'll go where I tell you to go. Next time be here when you're suppose to. Now take your post."

After roll call the young officer went around asking who had been given his assignment. He wanted it back and nothing was going to stop him from getting it. Who had his assignment? I did and I wasn't giving it up. When asked to relinquish it my answer was short and sweet. "No."

The assignment was a nice one, un-timed train patrol from 179th Street to Queens Plaza. I mean for a Transit cop on a Sunday it couldn't get much better. All I had to do was ride between the two stations, getting on and off whenever and wherever I wanted to. There wasn't a set time for me to be on any particular train or station. This was great. Free movement, if anyone wanted me they had to ask for my location over the radio.

Because he was late for roll call the young officer was given a fix station, Main Street on the #7 line in Flushing. That station sucked. It is a terminal station, the last stop. Every cop hates the terminal stations. All night long the train crews are calling for some drunk to be removed from the train. If not that, if something happened on the train while it was making its trip the crew would always report it when the terminal was reached. Something could have happened in Manhattan a different part of the city, an entirely different command. Unless it was serious the train crew would wait until they reached the terminal to report it. Gotta keep the trains moving.

A tour spent at one of these stations is going to be a long one. You don't get a break. A sleeper, a drunk, a fight, someone robbed, someone assaulted. Whatever, the calls just keep on coming. From the moment that an officer sets foot on a terminal station he or she is getting into something. The young officer can have it. More power to him this train patrol is fine with me.

As the night moves on I am enjoying the train runs. Northbound, southbound, get off wherever I want to, get on whenever I want to. I'm not responsible for the stations. There's other cops assigned to cover them. I'm the backup. If they need me I'm there. I got their back. It's a good day.

Around seven o'clock a call comes over for Main Street. Radio is calling for an officer to check on a sick passenger. The call is repeated four times. There's no answer from the young officer. A request is made for the Sergeant. "Sergeant who's covering Main street on the #7? We got a report of a man down, possible sick person," the radio operator said. Over the air I hear the shield and post of the young officer being called. "Keep calling him Central. Meanwhile I'll head over to check and advise," the Sergeant said.

Arriving at the station the Sergeant and his driver takes care of the sick person. He gives a final to Central asking, "Central did you get a response from the officer assigned to this station?" "No," the operator states. "10-4 Central, keep calling that officer every five minutes and let me know when you reach him."

For the next hour Central puts out the request for the officer, over and over again. No answer. Now things are getting serious. Not another missing officer, not this again. Where the hell is this guy I'm thinking. I know he was pissed off at the Sergeant and me also but that's no reason for him not to answer his radio. The broadcasts go on for another hour, still no answer. Where is this guy?

Central notifies the Sergeant that the Duty Captain had been informed of the missing officer. That's bad. Now the shit was hitting the fan. Wherever this cop was, whatever his reason for not answering his radio didn't mean squat now. The only thing that could save him from an ass ripping experience was if he was seriously hurt or dead. Anything short of these two excuses wasn't going to fly. That's it. The day was ruined.

Everyone on patrol had to phone in. "Where you at, have you seen officer so and so?" This went on throughout the city. No one had seen this officer no one knew where he was. Another search for a missing uniformed officer. All through the city cops were searching for him. Everything was negative.

Over the radio I hear a job for 169th street. Central reports some sort of disturbance. The radio states that there is a large crowd of people in a Transit Authority room, disorderly, playing loud music and drinking. The officers assigned to cover that station answer up. I tell Central that I will back them.

Hopping aboard a northbound train I'm only a few stations away, I'll be there in a couple of minutes. Reaching the station first the assigned officers was heard to cry out, "10/13! 10/13! Officer needs help 169th street, back end of station!" My train is only one station away. My heart starts to beat faster as again I hear, "10/13 Central! We have a large disorderly group 169th street." In the background of the transmission from the officer could be heard the voices of the group cursing and threatening the officers.

As my train pulled into the station my eyes searched the platform for any type of disturbance. Waiting for the doors to open seemed liked an eternity. Up the stairs I go running as fast as I can. I can hear yelling and screaming and the sound of approaching sirens. At the rear of the station is a large group of people. The two officers that had placed the call for help was surrounded by the mob, sticks in hand the officers stood back to back trying to fend off the angry mob.

Down the stairs swarms the troops. Cops jumping over turnstiles, rushing through the gates all headed for the mob. In the midst of the mob the two officers tried to fight their way out. From all sides they were now being hit. We had to save them. We had to stop the mob before they killed the officers.

In we go, sticks flying, mace being sprayed, punches being thrown, it's on now. This is a fight that we cannot lose, no way, no how. To lose this fight the mob would have to kill each and every one of us.

As I fought with one person, I could feel another grab for my gun. With that I slammed my elbow back as hard as I could, I made contact with someone's face. Smack right on the nose. Spinning away from the person behind me I'm hit on the side, there is no pain, just the feeling of being hit. My adrenalin is flowing full force.

With the arrival of more officers we are winning the battle. One by one the mob is taken down, the situation is coming under control. With the fighting over and the battle won everyone checks for wounds. Thank God no one is hurt badly, nicks and bruises only. The mob got the worst of it, some had to go to the hospital for treatment.

What had started this? What was the reason that we had to fight with these people? Why did things get so out of control? The answer was amazing. When the first two officers arrived at the station, they had found the room where the disorderly people were. Seems like the group wasn't really disorderly at that time, they were just having a party.

That's right they were partying their butts off in the subway. It was a birthday party. There were paper streamers hanging from the walls. There was food, drinks, presents and a cake. The party was in full swing when the officers arrived. Now who would be having a birthday party in the subway, who? That's right officer so-and-so.

When confronted by the investigating officers he reacted as if nothing was wrong. Trying to set him straight the two officers told him about the citywide search going on for him and how he was in big trouble. He had to shut the party down and return to the command.

Needless to say this did not go over big with the intoxicated officer or his crew. Cursing at the two officers that were now ruining his party he shouted, "Fuck you guys, get the hell out of here. If you don't leave I'll throw you out."

After making a move for one of his fellow officers the intoxicated officer was now being restrained. He cried out for help from the partygoers and the group moved in to eject the two officers holding their buddy from the party. Demanding that they let him go, the group confronted the officers.

Having no other choice they released their drunken coworker, who now called for the group to beat the living shit out of them. In their drunken loyalty they began to follow his charge. That's how this whole thing got started, by a stupid cop wanting to party instead of work. Not only party but also party while on duty, in uniform and off post.

The arrests were made, the ones with injuries taken to the hospital. Where's the cop? He's with the Captain. He's standing with his hands behind his back. Swaying from side to side he tries to keep from falling. The Captain is using words that would burn the ears of a sailor.

I noticed that the officer does not have a gun belt on and he has no shield. The Sergeant is holding them. "Give me," the drunken officer spits, "Give me back my shit!" With one hand the Sergeant pushes the officer back. "Just stand there, you stand there and be quiet. I don't want to hear anything from you!" Out comes the radio of the Captain, "Central be advised we have one member of the department under arrest at this time, please notify Internal Affairs." Placing his radio back in its holder without looking at the young officer the Captain states while walking away, "Get that piece of shit out of my sight!"

The Sergeant starts to walk the officer up the stairs. Led away in handcuffs in full uniform, damn that's bad. With the look of disgust on his face the Sergeant places the cop in the squad car. Needless to say this is now a former officer. His life ruined, his career down the drain, all for a party. The sight of him being taken away in cuffs is something I will never forget. This was indeed a vision that had to be remembered.

CHAPTER 26

▼

POWER TO BURN

Once a person decides that he or she is going to become a police officer they must realize that their entire life is going to change. The friendships that have been made throughout the years will be challenged. There are things that are done before accepting to wear a shield that can no longer be. Life must change and the sooner one realizes that the faster the transition will take place. For some, going through these changes the weeding out of the good from the bad will be easy. For others it will be the toughest thing they will ever have to do.

This vision concerns one such officer. A very popular guy the officer in question made friends quickly. He had something about him that just drew people to him. Tall, young, and handsome he didn't have a problem picking up girls. For him the subway was a huge hunting ground. With his silver tongue and good looks each day he would return from patrol with different names and phone numbers of the various girls he had charmed. This guy was good. He was the Romeo of the command. No one else even came close to matching his skills with the ladies.

The art of wooing was something he had learned while hanging with his boys. His crew could not be matched in their abilities to win over the hearts of young women. Many from the command would watch in amazement as the various young women came to meet the officer at the end of his shift. Seems he had a different girl for each day of the week and a different girl for each occasion.

The party life was still embedded in him. There's nothing wrong with going out and having a good time as long as you know where to draw the line. Since charming people came so easily for the young officer he thought he could talk his way into or out of anything. He was the so-called leader of his crew. Now that he was sporting a uniform, carrying a gun and shield, what could stop him? He was their God.

This officer had grown up in a rough part of the city where crime, drugs and alcohol were part of everyday life. This is where he met his crew, his friends and learned about life. When he made the decision to become a police officer his buddies scorned him at first. The crew he loved so much laughed at him and called him names. To them he was becoming a trader, going over to the other side.

For much of his training he was good. He had broken ties with his running buddies to focus on becoming a cop. However, being away from his buddies was not what he wanted. No, he longed to still be apart of their lives. As the months went past he was sailing through the academy picking up new skills that he would combine with his own street knowledge. He felt that he would be the best cop ever.

There was only one problem. He still yearned for his buddies. His heart would sink whenever he came across the guys doing what they did best, hanging out, picking up girls, and partying their butts off. The crew had not forgotten him. Each time they met the offer was made for him to return to them. They were sorry for the things that were said. Come back and join us. Oh, how he wanted to, but no. He had gone this far and he was not going to fall back now.

With the completion of the academy, he felt like he had accomplished a miracle. Moving forward in his chosen field was going to be great. Meeting new people, making new friends, letting go of the past. He made friends, with his gift it was not hard to do. The friends that he was making now though were of a different breed from what he was used to. Most of the officers were married, had kids, or had steady relationships. A more mature group of people. Going out with this new group was a bore. He tried his best to fit in with them but nothing worked. He needed his crew.

Putting hard feelings aside he rejoined his old buddies. The posse was together again. Nothing had changed. He slipped back into the groove like a key into a lock. He had become the perfect Dr. Jekyll and Mr. Hyde. By day he was the charming officer, a well-rounded person that seemed to have it all.

On the other hand by night he was a completely different person. Once the uniform came off he was still charming but not in a way to be proud of. The charm he used at work was to help people. To make them feel better about themselves, to comfort and also to better relations between the public and the police department. He used his powers for good.

Like a snake shedding its skin, once he peeled off the uniform a new image was brought forth. Falling back into the lifestyle he was supposed to be leaving behind, he found that with what he had learned in becoming a cop he had elevated himself into the master gangster.

With his posse in tow one flash of the badge and they would be granted entry to any club. The drinks would flow and the girls would come. Yes, he had the power he could do whatever he wanted. Whatever his posse needed he would furnish. He played the roll as leader to the hilt. Any problems that came about he took care of with his charm or with his badge.

There wasn't anything that could get in the way of his crew. Whatever they wanted they got, from little trinkets to larger objects, cars, women, clothing. With a flash of his smile, a flash of his badge and the show of his posse's muscle they were cleaning up. Wearing only the best clothing, driving the best car his power could get him. He was living large.

His posse took notice of how he had grown. How he got the best of everything. How he threw them the crumbs. Yeah, he was the leader. They were tight but things had to be made more even. Before there was no lion's share everyone got equally. So what if he's a cop, so what he got a shield, so what he got a gun. They all had guns. His was the only legal one but they all had guns. He was no better than the rest of them. Things had gotten to the point that they were now being treated like his lackeys. They were no longer on his level.

They had given him power as the leader. The crew had marveled at the things he could accomplish. His head had gotten too big. He had to be knocked down a bit. The crew tried to reason with their bigheaded leader. They were equal. Any and everything they got they were to share equally from now on. He could lead. They would give him his props but that was all they were going to give him, take it or leave it.

He left it. Who needed them? Not him, at one time he did but not anymore. Who was the one with the power? He was. They were just following him and feeding off his spoils. No he didn't need them they needed him. Feeling unstoppable he parted from his posse. They would need him before he needed them. Still up to speed he didn't miss a beat. Only the best clubs, wine, women, and rides for him. This time he did not have to share. Whatever he obtained he got to keep. No splitting, no listening to complaints of underlings, his bank was fat and getting fatter.

Members of his former posse took notice of his roll, with each change of car, with each change of women, they noticed. There wasn't much that he did that went unnoticed by the former posse. They were doing alright without him but they knew they could do much better with him. Getting into some of their favorite clubs was impossible without the flash of the shield. Obtaining the discounts and freebies they once enjoyed with him was no more. Maybe they did need him. Maybe it was better to follow in his shadows, feed off his crumbs and live the life of the rich and famous than to be just another group of wanna bees.

Putting pride aside the posse invited the former member back. All would be as it was. As if he was stepping on a roach he smashed the idea of him rejoining the crew. Tearing into the posse, the swollen headed cop told them where to go. What they could do with their offer. Like he had said before, they would need him before he needed them.

Being rejected was not a problem for the posse. But the way they were rejected was, yes it was a big problem. They had been dissed and they were going to get even. Bringing down a swollen headed cop isn't hard. With one phone call they got Internal Affairs attention. For weeks the different members of the posse recounted stories of their exploits. They told of the abuse of power. They told of the freebies and the discounts. The posse ventured into topics that uncovered a world of sex, drugs, and crimes.

Needless to say the IAB boys ate this stuff up. This rouge cop was going to be a feather in their caps. They followed the young bigheaded cop. Wherever he went he had a shadow. Whatever movement he made was closely watched. There wasn't a part of his life that went unchecked. His bank account and any transactions that he made were checked. His entire life was now under a microscope and he didn't know it. When he went shopping IAB was there. When he went to the bathroom IAB was probably there also. From what I've heard they can crawl up your butt and you wouldn't even know they were there.

As the months went by the members of the posse wondered why IAB had not taken him down yet. They had spilled their guts, telling everything to IAB. What was taking so long? The posse grew tired of waiting. They wanted him to fall and they wanted it now. How could they have been so stupid as to rat him out to IAB? Everyone knows cops take care of cops.

If they wanted to bring him down, to get even, they would have to take matters more into their own hands. The plan was simple they would call for a meeting with the cop. The posse would tell him that whatever he wanted was alright with them. They just wanted to be along for the ride. Whatever he threw their way was fine. The posse would fill his head with so much shit that he would have to take them back.

Accepting the offer of the posse for a meeting the cop arrived in his nice shinny car also he's wearing only the best. The posse greets him like it was old times. The group sit, talk and drink. Some also uses drugs. Feeling as if he is getting what he needs from the posse the cop agrees to take them back. It's party time for everyone. Bring on the girls and the music.

Outside IAB sits watching, waiting. The cop was playing right into their hands. All the time they had trailed him he had not made contact with the posse. By him being in the same apartment with them he was adding fuel to the fire that was going to burn him.

The music is pumping the drinks are flowing everyone is having a hell of a time. With each drink the cop is feeling more and more relaxed. Not noticing someone has lifted his gun from its holster the cop parties on. Drunker and drunker he gets, unable to stand he lies on a couch. The partygoers start to make their way out of the apartment, one by one they leave. Before the last posse member exits he pours gas on the floor around where the cop sleeps. A match is lit. The apartment goes up in flames.

From their car the IAB team sees the fire shoot out the windows. They rush inside the burning building in a vain attempt to rescue anyone that may be trapped. When the fire was put out there is only one victim to be removed. The body of the cop is taken out, placed in the back of an ambulance and taken away.

In the weeks that followed the members of the posse are rounded up. They knew it was coming. The posse knew they would have to answer for what had done to the officer. But they didn't care. When asked why the cop had been killed the answer was the same from each member. "No one disses us and gets away with it. We made him and we broke him. We gave you your shot! Fuck that motherfucker, let him burn in hell." The case was closed, and the posse went to jail. For the cop, I hope it was worth losing his life for wanting to be the king of New York.

At his funeral he had a closed coffin. There was no need for the world to see how bad of an end he had come to. There was a picture of him in uniform showing off his pearly white teeth. This is the way people would remember the flashy young man. He was a hero of the city, a hero to his family. This is how he was to be remembered.

To me he would be remembered as a heap of charred flesh. You see, I was stationed only one block away from the fire. When it erupted people ran to the subway screaming for help. Being one of the first responding officers to the scene I would get the chance to see what many others would not. Burned beyond recognition the body was removed from the building. It wouldn't be until later that I found out who it was. That is how I will remember the young officer. The vision of his charred body being placed into an ambulance, burned beyond recognition. That vision will stay with me for a very long time.

CHAPTER 27

▼

NEW YORK'S FINEST

All of the sights that came my way concerning the ups and downs of my fellow officers did not have to do with partying. Some of their falls came from having the wrong attitude towards the public. Seeing the fine people of New York as being lower then themselves lead to a quick and ungraceful end to the assuming officers.

Take for example one female officer, she not only thought that she was God's gift to this planet but also she saw herself as the finest of the fine. Taking great care in her appearance she would primp for what seemed like hours in the mirror before going out on patrol. Making sure each and every hair was in place. The makeup correctly spread upon her face, drenching her body with perfume she had to be perfect before going out to greet her public. How good she looked in her uniform, she thought. There could be no other female officer that came close to her.

Walking the platforms of the stations she covered, she moved with the grace of a runway model. With every step she took, her perfume would sail through the air catching the nose of anyone that happened to be nearby. When coasting about the inside of a train she would not miss an opportunity to check herself out in the windows. The sight of herself in the reflection only reinforced her opinion of herself.

Having to deal with the public only interrupted her day of self-gratification. Issuing a ticket was a chore. She calculated the way she held her pen. Too much pressure and she might break a nail. She couldn't have that. Griping the pen with so much care, she barely made readable marks on the ticket. Quite often the ticket was illegible. A single pen would last her for months.

The person that was receiving this notice of violation would have to wait for a significant amount of time before she was done. Rushing would endanger her nails. The chance of breaking one would increase if she were to speed up her writing. So if you ever had the misfortune of her issuing you a ticket you better had packed a lunch.

Having to get into a physical confrontation was unheard of for her. How could she place her hands on such trashy people. Just the idea of having to touch someone made her ill. The public was lucky that she graced them with her presence. Letting the public get a look at her was good enough. Having to place her hands on someone would be going too far. They did not deserve her touch.

Sometimes other young women would take note of how hard the young female officer worked to make sure everyone noticed how pretty she was. Comments of, "Who the hell does she think she is," was often heard. If not that there might be the old standby of, "What, she must think her shit don't stink." Whatever was said she had her come back ready, "Don't hate me because I'm beautiful, you could look like this too if you took better care of yourself." Most of the time this comment drew laughter. Sometimes it would lead to a full argument on what a beautiful woman really looks like.

The men were a different story all together. Watching as the female officer slinked down a platform or sashayed through a train, some would let out with catcalls. Others not impressed with her show would shake their heads or say things like, "You're trying to hard, shake it but don't break it." Even if the comments were negative she felt good. Why, because at least she got their attention. She must be doing something right.

For some guys that were lucky enough to come across her, she was to good to be true. They could not believe their eyes. This goddess of a woman was someone they had to meet, someone they had to throw the rap out to. Obtaining her phone number or having her possess theirs would be a high achievement, a feather in their cap. Having her at ones side would draw the admiration of many. With high hopes many guys tried to woo this vision of beauty, for to do so would prove their manhood.

Being rebuffed some admirers would walk away quietly feeling that at least they gave it a shot. Others weren't as nice. With words such as, "Who the hell do you think you are? Some kind of princess," or, "I was just trying to be kind, you look like you need it," they would share their displeasure with her. But the best response after being turned down had to come from a guy on a southbound #7 train. After making his move and being rejected by the female officer the young man took a step back and stated, "What you need is a good fucking, that'll straighten you out. Just one good fucking and you'll be alright." The entire train car exploded into laughter. I too could not help but to laugh.

Standing about twenty feet away from the female officer, I could see the look of shock that ran across her face. "How dare he," she must have thought, "How dare he talk to me like that." Having made his point the young man prepared to exit the train. People in the train car were still laughing at his verbal assault on the stunned officer.

With rage building up inside of her the young officer followed the male from the train. As the doors closed I could see her staring in his direction. What took place after the train left the station I'm not too sure of.

A few days later a call came into the command. Someone wanted to file a complaint on an unknown female officer that had attempted to mace him a couple of days in the past. The person had stated that he was followed by the officer and that for reasons he could not think of the officer had tried to mace him. He had done nothing to the officer and he wanted justice. Because he did not know the name or shield number of the officer there wasn't much that could be done. The complaint was taken and closed as, "Officer unknown."

I had not heard about the complaint until after it was closed. After hearing of the complaint I wondered, could that have been the female officer that was told off by her rejected suitor the other day? Could she have gone after him when they exited the train? This I didn't know. I had not seen her take any action towards the male. Maybe I was right, maybe I was wrong.

I spoke with the Sergeant about what I had seen and heard on the train and told him what I suspected may have taken place. I was told the complaint was closed and unless I had more information, unless I had actually seen her attempt to mace the guy, I should forget it, so I did. Time moved on and the female officer kept up with her routine. Playing to the public, primping at any chance she got she was on a roll.

Then came a night that she was ordered in for overtime along with eight other officers. She would be assigned to cover a station that the department had chosen as a hot spot for trouble. Each officer was given a station. There would be eight stations in a row blanketed by the Transit Police. The Street Cops would cover twelve blocks topside surrounding the stations. This was a sweep. Any and every violation or crime observed in the targeted area would be dealt with quickly. After putting on her best face at the command and checking herself out in the mirror, the female officer was ready for the night. She stood in her own corner of the train as we traveled to our assigned stations.

The rest of us talked and made meal plans with each other. The plan was that two officers at a time would be able to take meal. Officers on adjoining stations would be able to hookup with each other and eat together while watching each other's back. As the officers paired off I realized that my meal partner for the night was going to be the female that had distanced herself from us. My luck, I'm with Miss Thang, how was I going to hold my food down while sucking in all her perfume?

I informed her that she was to have meal with me and asked what kind of plans she wanted to make. Knowing the station I was going to be covering had the only open restaurant, I suggested that she travel to my station and we would have meal there. I should have known better. After telling her of my idea, she then gave me hers.

Head bouncing from side to side she suggested that I take her order now and when our mealtime comes up I go get her food then bring it to her. This would save her the trouble of having to walk across the dark street to get down to me. Giving me her money after placing her order she added, "And don't take too long getting here." I tucked her money in my pocket while under my breath I mumbled, "You bitch." Look, she is supposed to have my back tonight if something happens, so I couldn't say it to her face. I may have needed her for backup during the night and I didn't want to piss her off.

As the tour went along there wasn't much happening, no one was entering the station. A look up into the street also revealed nothing. What were we doing out here, not a thing is going on, the subway and the streets were quiet. On the station covered by the female officer, things were going along about the same. She had taken up a position sitting on a turnstile across from the token booth. Sitting and reading a magazine she let the time slip by.

The clerk spent his time checking out the officer. He watched her every movement. She was such a pretty sight to have on a long night. Deep in thought as to how to start up a conversation with her, he let his mind fantasize about her. There must be a good opening line that he could use. Maybe a joke, no maybe a comment on how good she looks. No, those were probably lines she heard all the time. He had to come up with something better.

Watching the officer sitting on the turnstile, his eyes went from her head down her body to her feet, then back up again. When she stood up to shake out her legs, his eyes that were fixed upon her took in every movement she made. He could not take his eyes off her.

Glancing towards the booth she notices him looking at her. She smiles at him. He perks up. "She gave me a smile," he thinks, "That's good." Taking this as his opening, he waves her over. Gliding across the mezzanine she approaches the booth. With his eyes still fixed on her, the clerk is getting his rap in order. Leaning against the booth she bows her head and ask, "What can I do for you?" Without hesitating the clerk responds, "I just wanted to know if you're married? A pretty woman like you shouldn't be alone." Stiffening her back the officer stands up while mouthing back, "You gotta be kidding me, why would I waste my time on you? Get real!" Taken back by her response, the clerk sat back in his chair, stunned.

Watching as the female returned to her perch his opinion of her had changed. "She must be kidding me, she's nice but she's not all that," he thought. "Look I was just trying to be nice," he spoke over his microphone, "Since we both gotta be here I thought we might as well get along." Without lifting her head from her magazine she paid him no attention. Even though she had such a bad attitude the clerk still found her appealing. He didn't want to but he couldn't help himself. "Later for her," he thought, "She can't stop me from looking." So he did. He couldn't take his eyes off of her.

In front of the booth appears a man blocking the view of the clerk, "Can I go in?" he asks. "You gotta ask the Cop," the clerk replies. The man makes his way over to the female officer, "Excuse me, I don't mean to bother you but I don't have any money, and I was wondering if you could let me go in?" There's no answer from the officer, so again the man makes a request to be let into the station. Again he gets no response.

Feeling he's being ignored the man reaches out to tap the officer on the shoulder. "Get your hands off of me," she fires out, "Don't you put your hands on me!" Now rising to her feet she stands in front of the man. The clerk hears her say, "Who the hell do you think you are? You don't know me, don't touch me, you better get the hell away from me." Not wanting any trouble the man apologizes for touching the officer. He says, "I just wanted to get your attention. I want to know if it's ok if I go in through the gate cause I got no money." With the venom of a snake the officer gives the man a stern answer of, "No! Now get away from me, start walking."

Shaking his head while walking away the male zings back a remark of, "Fuck you bitch," to the officer. Springing from the turnstile she shouts, "What did you call me?!!" Feeling frisky the male again states, "Fuck you bitch." With her fury building the officer reaches for her gun, "No one talks to me like that!" she screams. "I got your bitch right here!"

Seeing the officer now with her gun in hand the male turns to run. "Take that bitch!" the officer yells while letting loose a shot. The bullet ricochets off the floor of the mezzanine and heads toward the fleeing man. As he turns to go up the stairs the bullet digs into his left butt cheek.

Seeing but not believing what he's seeing the clerk hits the emergency alarm in the booth. He picks up the phone and calls in that a cop's in trouble. "10-13," blurs over the radio, "Officer needs help." I listen for the location, "Oh shit, that's the next station down, that's the female I'm supposed to be backing up tonight."

Away I go with my heart pumping faster now. Over the radio comes, "From the railroad clerk, report of shots fired, man down." As I exit the train running along the platform, I could hear the voices of other officers asking, "What happened, what happened, are you hurt?" I put over my radio, "We got the officer, no further officers needed."

Looking to my left I could see the man laying at the foot of the stairway, blood coming from his rear. He's handcuffed and moaning. The female officer is standing near the turnstiles. She doesn't seem to be fazed by shooting the man. As I go over to her I hear another officer ask her, "What happened, did he have a gun? Why did you shoot him?" With a calm voice she replies, "No one calls me a bitch! That'll teach him!" With her hand on her hip and head moving from side to side she adds, "Now he'll be more careful who he calls a bitch!"

Needless to say that was the end of that officer's career. She was arrested and fired. The man later filed a lawsuit against her and the department. The officer was found guilty and sent to jail.

For me the sight of her being placed in the rear of a patrol car and taken away while still cursing out the male hoping for someone to take her side was pitiful. How could she let him get away with calling her a bitch? She didn't do anything wrong, he deserved what he got. That was her attitude. Why didn't we understand? This sight was bad. The vision of a pretty young woman lost in her own vanity now on her way to jail would also stay with me for a long time.

CHAPTER 28

▼

TORMENTED

Youth is not the only burden that is carried by officers. Far from it, youth as we have seen can lead to the destruction of a person if he or she cannot or will not move into adulthood and maturity. With the advancement into adulthood one is thought to be able to think more clearly, to be able to recognize wrong from right. One should be able to make the tough decisions on some hard topics that life will throw at them. Yes, a grown adult is thought to be able to make these decisions. Hopefully they will make the correct ones. But what happens when the wrong decision is made? What could be the outcome? Lets look at one such case.

With many years under his belt as a police officer roaming the streets of the city and covering the vast subways, this officer seemed to have passed the test of time. He was professional in his approach. He had what many thought to be a stable life. There were no problems at work. His private life never came into question. He was the type of officer everyone enjoyed working with. Whatever the situation that arose he could handle it. No one knew of the demons that were following him, no one knew of the monkey that was on his back. Looking back had I known, perhaps there was something I could have done to help him fight off his tormentor.

Slipping into roll call the officer took a seat in the rear of the room. This was a little odd, as he always sat in the front. Sitting in the seat beside him I got the whiff of alcohol, it was coming from the officer. "Rough night?" I asked while fanning away the strong odor that was being emitted by the officer. "What you mean by that?" he said.

Not wanting to give the impression that I was being nosey, I responded with, "You look tried, that's all, thought maybe you were out late." Popping a stick of gum into his mouth the officer told me to mind my own business. No problem, he was a veteran he had been on the job for a lot longer time then I had. Also he was old enough to be my father. Who was I to question him?

As roll call went on the Sergeant called everyone to attention, he was going to do an inspection. This was rare, we were inspected maybe three times a year at the most. Making his way around each officer the Sergeant looked for proper grooming, uniform and polished shoes. He moved quickly from one to the other. Everything was looking well, and then he stopped in front of the older officer that was standing to my right.

Giving him a good going over, the Sergeant could find nothing wrong with the officer's appearance. Before moving on to me the Sergeant told the older officer, "See me after roll call." As the Sergeant checked me out I wondered if he had also smelled the scent of booze on the older officer and if he had noticed the look of fatigue on the officer's face. After giving me the once over the Sergeant dismissed us.

Into the office he and the officer went. Door closed, the two were in the office for two to three minutes when voices were raised. "You don't come to work in that condition. I'm responsible for turning you out fit for duty. If something happens to you out there, it's my ass on the line! What the fuck is wrong with you coming in here smelling like a brewery? If you got a problem I suggest you get some help." The words came out strong and loud from the Sergeant. He was not going to let the officer put him in jeopardy.

"Give me your gun and shield!" the Sergeant demanded. "Give them to me and go home, I'll see you tomorrow and you better not come in looking the way you did today!" With the words of, "Fuck you, you can have my shit, come take it! I'll like to see you try," the officer cut into the Sergeant, "You want my gun, I'll give it to you, how you want it bullets first!" The situation in the office was getting out of control.

The Sergeant yelled out for assistance. Rushing into the office I saw the older officer holding his gun in his right hand, with a firm grip the weapon shook from side to side. Eyes fixed on the Sergeant, the officer spat out, "Here it is take it, you said you wanted it so take it!"

Trying my best not to upset the officer further I said, "Just put the gun down. Whatever the problem is that's not going to help. Just put the gun down." Praying that he would listen to me, hoping that a tragedy was not going to take place, I stuck out my hand for the gun. For what seemed to be an eternity I waited, praying all along that he would give me the gun.

Placing the gun into my hand the officer spat at the Sergeant, "You don't know me, you don't know anything about me. That's alright you can take all my shit. I don't need it anyway." Once the gun was secured other officers grabbed the cop. Holding him by his arms he was led out of the office. A call was placed for an ambulance to respond to the command. The officer was removed to the hospital for evaluation. He was suspended and departmental charges were drawn up on him. Unfit for duty, insubordination, being drunk on duty and threatening the life of a superior officer, was how the charges read.

A week had passed by since the officer was suspended, no one had heard from him. He had not been seen. I wondered if he was ok. When I called his home I received no answer. Stopping at his home after work I got no answer at his door. He must not want to talk. Maybe he's alright, maybe he just needs time I told myself. Driving away I happened to spot the officer standing in front of an off track-betting parlor. Stopping my car I called out to him, he looked in my direction and said nothing.

Out of the car and over to the suspended officer I went. "Hey, you ok, you alright?" I asked. Without even looking at me, he told me to get the fuck away from him. "Look, I'm just trying to see if there's something that I can do for you, if I can help." Again he told me to get the fuck away from him, only this time adding, "How the hell can you help me? No one can help me, now go away." With that said, I left. He didn't want my help, he didn't want to talk, what could I do? I had made an effort, he turned me down, there was nothing more I could do.

Months went by and there was no mention made of the officer. He would only be seen on paydays when he came in to pick up his check. Even though he was suspended he was still being paid. Into the command he would come retrieve his check and leave without saying a word to anyone. This went on for weeks.

Then one night as I sat at the desk position to assist the Sergeant a call came in. It was the precinct that covered the suspended officers house. The voice was somber, the officer on the other end of the line wanted to know if we had an officer so-and-so assigned to the command. "Yes we do, but he's not working now," I said, "Is there something I can help you with?" I inquired.

Stuttering for a moment the cop on the other end of the phone stated, "Look, we found your guy in the street, he shot himself, he's dead." Taken back by what I was told I looked at the Sergeant saying, "You better take this." I sat and watched as the Sergeant was told about the officer. Hanging up the phone, his face flush the Sergeant stated, "Let's go, that son of a bitch killed himself."

Arriving at the scene of the officer's death I could see his body still lying in the street. Covered by a sheet, he was laying head first in the street, feet on the sidewalk. Over to us steps a detective, "We found this in his pocket," holding out the officers ID card, "We also found this," producing a crumpled piece of paper, he unfolded it.

As the Sergeant and I read the suicide note we shook our heads. With the feeling of wanting to cry I read on. The note told of how the officer had become hooked on gambling. It told of how he had lost his car, his home and his family. Each paycheck went to his bookies or to off-track betting. Reading on, the note told of how he had fallen into drinking and drugs to ease the pain and the shame he was feeling. For the last nine months he had been sleeping in the streets, the subway or a shelter.

He told of the pain that he had inflicted on his family. He told of how sorry he was, how he never wanted any of this to have taken place. He wanted to make things right, for him there was only one way to do that. He had to stop hurting the people that he loved. He had to free himself from the demons that had taken control of him. Taking his life would do that, so he did. The officer ended his note with, "Please tell my family I'm sorry. I'm sorry for everything. I do love them but I don't love myself, I'm sorry."

After finishing the note I handed it back to the detective. There I stood watching as the officer's body was placed into the ambulance. The blood soaked sheet that had covered him lay in the street. As the months went on and life returned to normal, sometimes I would think back to what I had seen that night. The vision of a dead officer laying in the gutter, his life fluids going down into the sewer was a hard thing not to remember. I would see this vision everyday for a very long time.

CHAPTER 29

▼

YOU MAKE THE CALL

Moving through my career, there were times I thought I had seen all the bad things possible. After seeing the visions that you too now have witnessed I felt as though I had seen just about everything. How could the visions get any worse? How wrong I was for there were more to come. More visions that made the others pale in comparison.

Take for example the following. A new class had graduated from the academy, three hundred new officers that needed to be shown the ropes of the road. Training new officers was not an assignment that I looked forward to. After working most of the time by myself, having to carry someone around with me all day was not what I wanted.

As the new officers came into the command they were sized up by us, not wanting to be stuck with someone I considered to be a know-it-all or a knuckle head, I questioned the officers. "What did you do before you went into the academy? Why did you become a cop? From what you've learned in the academy do you think you can do this job?" Depending on how these questions were answered I would make a decision on whom to work with.

You see, the department wanted to keep the veteran officers happy and also give the new officers the chance to work with someone that was going to train them the right way. By doing this, the department would also be keeping the young officers happy by giving them the best training officers possible.

After going about my question and answer session, I decided upon a young female officer. She seemed to have a good head on her shoulders and was eager to learn. Asking questions and watching closely on how I went about my patrol she was picking up a lot of knowledge.

She was an easygoing person and we got along well, it felt like I had a mini-me at my side. Like a hand in a glove we fit together well. I learned her movements and she learned mine. If there was a condition to be handled we took care of it in a smooth way, no problems, no stress, this was working out great. How could I have picked a better person to work with? I couldn't.

During the days we would talk about each other's lives. I told her about my family, about how I became a cop, about what I thought of the job, and how I felt the job thought about me. Taking in what I said and offering her opinions she kept the day moving along well. When I would finish with my topics she would start with hers.

She was not married, had no kids and had only recently moved out from her mother's house into her own apartment. She told of how when she was growing up, she always wanted to be a cop. Her favorite television shows were all cop shows. When she played cops and robbers as a kid, she would always be the cop. Telling of how she wanted to be a detective like Starsky and Hutch or maybe Cagney and Lacey, she would take me step by step through how she wanted her career to go.

This kid was smart. She knew when to speak up and when to keep quiet. The job came naturally to her. As the weeks of training went on, I knew that she was going to be alright. She had what it took to get the job done. I was proud to have shared my knowledge with her. When the training was completed we parted, solo patrol is the normal thing in transit.

Once in a while we would bump into each other either in the command or out on the road. Whenever we did come across each other we would exchange greetings and ask how each other was doing. Once when I bumped into her, she told me how happy she was, that she had met and was now dating a fellow officer.

As she spoke of her new boyfriend her eyes would light up, her voice would be that of a schoolgirl talking about her first crush. From the way she spoke of him, he seemed to be the perfect guy for her. The two had met at a softball game between our command and his.

She told of how he was a tall, good-looking guy who she thought could have his pick of the ladies but he had chosen her. She felt lucky that he had picked her and hoped that he felt the same way about her, she was sure he did. Telling her how happy I was for her I gave her my best wishes. This would be the last time I saw the female officer for four months.

Then came the day that I was checking over the assignment sheet, there was her name. Why was she on my tour, was this a mistake? I asked the Sergeant, he told me that it was correct. The officer was now assigned to my tour. I thought this was fine, a person that I could talk to, not just bullshit with if we were teamed up on a station.

Suited and waiting for roll call to begin, I watched as the other officers filed into the muster room. Knowing that the female officer would be entering soon, I saved her a seat next to me. I wanted to show her that she was welcomed on her new tour and also that I had not forgotten her. Into the room walked the officer. Her uniform was still looking new. She still had the look of a rookie.

I called to her, "Hey rookie, come sit over here." As she turned to the sound of my voice I observed that she was wearing dark sunglasses. A smile formed on her lips as she answered me by saying. "Ok Pop's I'll sit by you, looks like you could use the company." As we sat talking about the good old times I wondered as to why she was wearing the sunglasses. "I got an eye infection and the doctor told me to keep bright lights out of my eyes for a while." Her answer flew with me, it sounded right. "Other then that, how have you been?" I inquired, "Is everything alright, how's that young man of yours?"

Her answer was short and to the point, "I'm fine and so is he, enough about me lets talk about you. How you been doing?" Not one to talk about myself much, the conversation was over quickly. As we sat quietly awaiting for roll call to begin, I noticed that she kept fixing the sunglasses, making sure that they were on properly. For the next twenty minutes she didn't say a word, she sat and stared. Thinking maybe she didn't want to be bothered I said nothing. She must have a lot on her mind. If I had only known then what I know now, maybe, just maybe I could have helped her.

As the days went by she grew more and more into herself. She was not the same young woman that I had known. There was something wrong. Something that was having a devastating affect on her. What was taking place in her life, I did not know. She would not open up. She would not seek out assistance. I watched as this bright and happy person withdrew into a shell, becoming a shadow of what she was. What could be changing her so, what problems were she having that was tearing her apart? One day while on my way to the command I would get a clue.

After parking my car I headed towards the command. There on the corner stood the female officer, she was having an argument with some guy. As I got closer to the couple, I heard her say, "Why do you treat me like this, what have I done to you?" The guy tried to walk away but she held him by his arm. Pulling away from her grasp he said, "I told you, if you do what I want there would be no problem. You're the one that make me do the things I do. If you act right then I'll treat you right."

Not wanting the two to lose control I intervened, "What's up, you guys got a problem, what's the matter?" The young man said nothing, and the female insisted that everything was fine. She then introduced me to the young man. We shook hands. But before I released his hand, I gave it a squeeze, while looking him straight in the eyes I said, "You know, we think a lot of this young officer, you better be treating her right, know what I mean." After giving his hand another hard squeeze I released him. We stood looking at each other for a few seconds before he stated, "You got it man, whatever she wants." "I'll talk to you later," he snared at the young officer before walking away.

As we walked to the command I noticed a bruise on the young officer's face. "Did he do that?" I said. Covering the bruise with her hand she replied, "It's alright, he didn't mean it." Stopping her before she could go any further I offered, "Look, if this guy is putting his hands on you, you don't have to take it. You know better than that. If he's doing that to you now, what's he going to do to you later? If you don't stop him now he's only gonna get worst." Looking up at me she just said, "I'm alright, I can handle it."

Knowing deep down inside that she was not going to take any action towards correcting her boyfriend's behavior, I decided to speak with the peer counselor of the command. Pulling him aside I told of what I had observed and heard. His response to me was, "If she doesn't ask for help, there's nothing we can do, understand." Yeah, I understood in other words mind your own business.

The days came and went. The female officer said nothing. It seemed that she went out of her way to avoid me. Checking the assignment sheet one day I noticed that I was assigned a two-officer station. My partner for the night would be the female officer. This was perfect I thought. She might not talk in the command but being together for eight hours I'll get her to open up. I waited for her at roll call. She should be coming in any moment now. There's no way for her to get out of talking with me. She had to. For eight hours I would question her. I'll get her to open up.

Roll call starts, she's not present. The Sergeant calls her name, no answer. A check in the locker room, she's not there. He asked at the desk if maybe she had been excused for the day. The answer is no.

The desk officer says he will call her house and see if he can reach her. Before he is able to place the call, the Sergeant from the day tour tells him that some guy had called in for the female officer and tried to get an excusal for her. He told the guy that he would have to speak to the officer in order to grant her an excusal. This was not to be, the guy on the phone said that she was in the bathroom and that he would have her call back.

Not thinking much about the call he had put it out of his mind. Upon hearing that the female did not show up for work, he now thought that maybe something was wrong. "Check the sick list," the Sergeant said. No, she's not out sick. "Ok call her house again," the Sergeant says. The call is placed, no answer. "Alright you come with me," the Sergeant says to me, "I want you to drive me over to her house, we'll get to the bottom of this."

As we arrived at the female's apartment house we saw fire trucks in front. "What's up?" I inquired. The super called in a smell of gas coming from apartment 14c. He knocked but no one answered. As the smell got stronger he decided to call the fire department. Wait, did he say apartment 14c? That's the female officers apartment.

Up the stairs we go, the sense of urgency was high. The fire department had gained entry to the apartment and the smell of gas filled the rooms. Watching and waiting from my position in the hallway I waited for someone to say everything was alright, that she wasn't inside.

This was not to be. A fireman steps into the hallway and says, "You guys say there's a cop that lives here?" "Yeah," I said, "Is she in there?" Moving his head from side to side the fireman says, "Yeah, she's in there, but she's dead."

Rushing inside I see the body of the young officer lying on the floor of the kitchen. She is naked, there is blood coming from her head. On the floor next to her is a gun, her off duty, a five shot Smith and Wesson. The oven door is open and the smell of gas is going away. The young officer is dead. Shot once in the head.

Damn this sucks. Why would she kill herself, why would she do it? The investigation by the police department would answer their questions but for me it would create some.

First of all, if someone fires a revolver there should be gunpowder on that person's hand, if they are not wearing gloves. The female officer did not have gunpowder on her hands and remember she was naked.

My second question was, how did the bullet that was fired from her gun leave its spent shell on the bottom of the cylinder? When fired, the cylinder of the gun should have turned only once to the next chamber, not spin to the bottom.

My third question was, how come there were no fingerprints found on the gun? Not the female officers, no ones. Was it wiped clean? How could she shoot herself and not leave fingerprints on the gun?

Over the years no one answered these questions. The death of the young officer was labeled a suicide. With all types of clues that suggested to the contrary, it was still closed out as such.

At the funeral of the young female her boyfriend was not there. He had to work, couldn't make it. I found out later that he had been investigated as to his whereabouts when the female officer was killed. That investigation went nowhere because he had a good excuse, he was on patrol far away from her apartment at the time of her death. His alibi was solid and no one could prove differently.

Only two people know what happened in that apartment that night. The two people that know what took place, as far as I'm concerned, are the person that killed the young officer, if that's what happened and the young officer herself. She can't give any answers and the other isn't talking. Was this a suicide or not, that question still haunts me.

CHAPTER 30

▼

THE UNKNOWN

The visions of tragedy came and went. Each week brought a new course of events. Starting out each tour I had no idea what would await me. Adventure was not missing at all. Just stepping out the door of the command could be an adventure. Let us drift back to a cold snowy February. The day was brisk. Outside temperature was about twenty degrees. With the wind chill the temperature stood at a bone chilling five below zero. Oh yeah, it was cold. Brutal is more like it, just plain brutal.

With the city streets blanketed in snow most travelers took to the subways, making for larger crowds than normal. I myself chose to use the steel beast for transport, not wanting to dig out my car from home. Because I did not want to go slipping and sliding through snowy streets to reach the job and then have to dig out a parking spot once I got there. No, I'll just leave the car, might as well start the day off right. Why put off entering the hole? I was going to be stuck in it all day anyway. Maybe that's why I wanted to put it off, because I was going to be stuck in it all day. I hated using the subway to get to and from work it just made the day longer.

Boarding the train at the station closest to my home was no easy task. Each car of the trains was packed, jammed from front to rear. Standing room only or should I say squashing room only. Letting four trains go by without attempting to board, I had no choice but to get on the next one.

In comes the train, yeah that's right jammed, when the doors opened, the people inside were so thick I didn't think a sheet of paper could fit into the car. Turning my back to the crowd I began pushing my way in, resistance was futile, I was getting on, come hell or high water. Crammed up against the door, arms pinned at my sides there I stood.

There wasn't a need to hold onto anything because the crowd was holding me up. If the train rocked or shook I didn't move, no one moved. The body heat generated by the people made the train feel like it was the middle of summer. Sweat and funk had taken over the train. Damn it was funky in there. After suffering through my ride I made it to the command, sticky and worn out. I felt like I had already put in a full days work, what a way to start the day.

Roll call was late. It had to be, because the majority of the officers were late. After waiting for thirty minutes, the Sergeant told everyone present to go and make their way to post. Out the door we stepped, five out of fifteen officers, what a turn out.

As I stood on the northbound platform awaiting the train, I was amazed at how many people were on the station. This wasn't rush hour. I knew the trains were crowded but this was overload. As the trains came and went I waited, unable to board. I tried the front of the trains, I tried the middle and the rear, no luck I couldn't get on.

Boarding a train in uniform is different from boarding while in civilian clothing. I have to protect my gun, stick, mace, and cuffs. Everything on my gun belt had to be secured, and a crowded train made this very difficult.

So I waited and waited. The trains came in and the trains went out. I stood and watched each and every one of them. This was not going to be easy. Here I am forty minutes out the door and I have not even gone one station. Making my way to what looked like a better spot to attempt my boarding, I headed towards the front of the station. The next train that came in was mine no one was going to stop me from getting on.

It's cold as hell and I need some coffee. The warmth that had been in my boots had gone and the frost was taking over. That's it, no way I'm gonna let my feet freeze. Once my feet go I'm finished, I'll be screwed for the rest of the day. With my mind made up, I was going to do whatever it took to get on the next train.

As the doors opened I was taken back for a moment. The car wasn't packed with people there was plenty of room. I got lucky. I had out waited the crowds. Stepping through the doors of the train, I found out why the car was empty.

There wasn't any heat. The damn car was colder than it was outside. Frost came from my nose and mouth with each breath and my feet got colder. Looking around the car, I observed several people wrapped in thick winter coats, hats pulled over their ears. They sat in this refrigerator like nothing, just meat in cold storage. Well not me, into the next car I go leaving that icebox behind.

Opening the door to the second car I couldn't wait to feel the heat. Damn, it's just as cold in here as it was in the other car. What's up with this? On I go. I had to find a car with heat. Through the third, fourth, fifth cars I traveled, still no heat. Keep moving, one of the cars must have heat, I kept saying to myself. As I approached the sixth car I could see that the number of people inside had increased. There was the heat. No way all those people would be in that car unless the heat was on.

Squeezing my way inside, I could feel the warmth invade my body. That is what I was looking for. This was the spot. I stood in my own little corner, sucking up as much of the heat that I could. When the train pulled into the next station the doors did not open right away. I waited along with the others, knowing that once the doors did open there would be a release from the crush. When the doors finally did open I stepped out. As I looked to my left observing the exiting passengers, everything seemed normal.

Then all of a sudden I saw a large group of people running towards me. Those people were hauling ass, full out sprinting at break neck speed. "What the hells going on?" I wondered, "What are they running from, what's back there?" Before I could move, I heard the conductor calling for me to come to his position. Clutching my stick in hand I started making my way through the fleeing crowd. "What's going on?" I asked as they breezed past me. "What's happening back there?" No answer, just people yelling and screaming. Some were pointing but not giving an answer as to what was happening.

My mind, not wanting to fix on any one thought, kept bouncing between the possible and the impossible. "Stay focused," I told myself, "Keep yourself ready for anything." The people are still flashing by me. Some are falling to the ground others are stepping on the fallen ones. This is madness. "What the hell is going on back there," I thought. No one told me anything or gave me a hint.

Slowing my pace I observed the conductor, he's standing outside the last car. With his arms waving like a windmill he urges me on. Calling out, "Back here, it's back here, hurry up," he yells at me. "What, what's going on?" I yell back, "What you got?" He didn't answer he just kept waving his arms repeating, "Back here, it's in here."

As I reached the conductor I told him, "Calm down and tell me what's going on?" He points inside the last car stating, "There's some kind of thing, I don't know what it is. They told me that it bit some people, it's in there." Again I asked, "What? What the hell is in there, did you see it?" With his eyes bugging out and his hands shaking he said, "I think I saw something but I'm not sure what it was, it went over there," pointing towards the far corner of the car.

Trying my best to get a look at whatever it was in the train, I peered through the windows. No luck, I couldn't see a thing. Back and forth I moved along the outside of the train car, hoping for a sight of whatever it was that had sent an entire train of people fleeing for their lives.

Central is calling, they want to know what's going on. I don't know what to tell them. There's something going on but I don't know what. "Unit, unit at the scene give me an update of your condition. Do you need additional personnel?" Not knowing what to say I came back with, "Central, be advised, I've been informed by the conductor that there is some kind of animal aboard the train, report of people bitten, I need additional units and animal control." "Unit what type of animal do you have there? A dog, what type of animal is it?" the radio operator presses me for details. "When I find out, I'll let you know Central," I responded.

Still unable to spot whatever it was inside the train I came up with a brainstorm of an idea. To this day I don't believe what I did but yes, I did it. Telling the conductor to key open one of the closed doors so that I would be able to enter I prepared myself to go in. Pulling on my gloves was step one. Getting a good firm grip on my stick was step two. I'm ready.

I tell the conductor to open the door and leave it open. I'll make my way inside to check out the condition. My last words to him were, "Do not close this door, I may need to get out fast, understand!" Telling me he understood, that he wouldn't close the door, the conductor stood ready. "Ok open it," I said. With a quick turn of his key the door slid open.

Slowly I stepped inside, looking for any sign of movement. Giving the conductor a look of reassurance I started to move forward. Heart pumping a mile a minute, I'm wide eyed on the alert for my prey. Then I saw it, a long narrow tail sticking out from the corner of the last seat. "What kind of tail is that?" I think, "It's not a dog, what is it?"

Well I wouldn't have to wait long to find out what it was. As I watched the tail, all of a sudden it disappeared, out pops the biggest rat I've ever seen in my life. Without hesitating I leaped onto the bench seat, stick in hand waiting to be attacked. I thought, you gotta get out of here, damn that thing is big.

Then I heard it, the sound of the door closing, that damn conductor had locked me inside with the fucking rat. A turn of my head towards the door and I could see that, I was trapped. I could see the conductor looking at me. I started yelling at him, "Why the hell did you close the door? Open the fucking door now, let me out of here!" Shaking his head from side to side he gave me the answer I didn't want, "No way, I can't let that thing get out. Shoot it, you got a gun, just shoot it."

Now there's an idea, shoot the rat. It sounded good except for one thing. If I shot the rat, I'm most likely to be suspended for improper use of my weapon. Shoot the rat and get suspended or don't shoot the rat and get bit. What a choice I had. Screwed no matter which choice I made. There's got to be another.

The rat is advancing on my position. I swing my stick at it, trying to keep it away. Man this thing is huge. It's the size of a small dog and I don't mean a very small dog. By small I mean a small pit bull, if there is such a thing.

Outside the train now I see a group of officers staring at me. They're yelling stuff like, "Round 'em up cowboy," or "Yo rat man we got the rat signal." Trying my best to ignore my fellow officers, I started making my way along the seats. With each step that I took the rat made a jump up towards me. Swinging my stick with full force at the leaping rat I kept making my way towards the rear of the train. No help is coming from my fellow officers. No, they're enjoying the show.

As I reached the last seat, I'm cornered. I can go no further. The rat is about five feet away from me, it's getting closer, what the hell am I gonna do now? Looks like I'm gonna have to shoot this damn thing. Out comes the mace, squeezing the trigger I empty the can. It had no effect. The damn rat just shook off the mace. I threw the empty mace can at it. The can bounced off of the rat without doing any harm. Now what, what the hell am I going to do now? I can't shoot this rat, what am I going to do?

Like a bolt of lighting an idea hits me. I motion for the conductor to come to the rear storm door. I tell him to just unlock the door and move back. "Can you do that?" I asked, "Just unlock the door I'll do the rest." Thank God, he listened to me. I watched as he unlocks the door.

Now it's my turn, down from the seat I go, stick swinging as fast as possible. I clip the rat on its head, he moves back. I reached for the door and slid it open. Swinging my stick again at the rat while moving forward, I started heading it towards the door. Giving one final leap the rat flashing its teeth lunges up at me. Like Babe Ruth, I gave a mighty swing of my stick, contact, a mid body strike.

The force of the swing sends the rat flying through the open door onto the tracks. It lands and to my amazement rolls to its feet and runs into the darkness.

The officers, the conductor and the passengers that were watching this show all burst out laughing. Me, I was just relieved that it was over. So I thought. Yes the rat was gone, I wasn't hurt and I also found out that it had not bitten anyone, that's great. Just put over the radio that the rat is gone, no paperwork, looking good.

Not with my luck, I spent the rest of my day filling out aided reports. Sixty aided reports on the people that got injured falling over each other as they ran from the killer rat. Believe me the ranking that I took from the other officers about that rat will probably go down in history. I don't know if you have ever seen a subway rat, I had seen plenty of them but nothing like the one that chased me around that train car. That rat holds a special vision in my mind.

CHAPTER 31

▼

CO-WORKERS

Taking in the vast sights of the subway gave me something to look forward to each day. Going to work, I knew something awaited me. I just had no idea what it was. Every day was different. There was no such thing as a typical day.

For a while I was assigned to work undercover, plainclothes is what the cops call it. Working in plainclothes opened up a whole new world of sights. Mixing in with the riding public while in my civilian clothes I could see things that I never could while in uniform. Earlier I gave you a taste of a plainclothes vision with my tale of the female beggar. Now I will give you a chance to witness a sight unseen by most.

My partner and I were assigned to cover a station where a rash of purse snatchings had been taking place. This was a small station, only one token booth. The mezzanine was only thirty feet by twenty feet, a close contact area. There was hardly enough room to stretch your arms. Having only one exit made covering the station easy. All we had to do was to watch the mezzanine and the platforms.

If any crime were to take place, the perpetrator had to flee past us. Taking up our positions, me on the mezzanine, my partner on the platform, we were ready, bring it on. We had this station on lockdown. The time went by slowly, nothing was happening. Only drips and drabs of people entered and exited, this was going to be a long day.

As I sat on the last step of the stairway leading to the street, a thought crossed my mind. Here we are staking out this station waiting for someone to snatch a bag, waiting to put an end to this crime spree. We didn't know who we were looking for. All we knew was that the guy doing the crimes was about six feet tall and wore dark clothing.

The victims were unable to give good descriptions of the male because he always struck from the rear. He would come up from behind his victims, snatch their pocketbooks and keep on running out the station. The only part of the perpetrator that was seen by the victims was his backside, so they couldn't give a good description.

The problem that I was having was trying to figure out why the booth clerk never got a good look at this guy. In fleeing the station he had to run right past the booth. It seemed almost impossible that the clerk could not have gotten a look at him. Each time a crime had taken place and the clerk was asked if he had seen anything he replied, "No." He wasn't paying attention, he had his head down, was in the toilet or straightening up the booth. Each time the clerk saw nothing.

Now I'm thinking to myself, "If I was the clerk and some guy is ripping off people on my station, I would be keeping a close eye on everyone that came in or went out. I would want this guy caught as soon as possible." My thinking would be, "Hey, if he gets away with robbing the passengers what's to stop him from robbing the token booth." Even if I didn't care much about the other people that were robbed, I would have to care about myself. Wanting this guy caught would be at the top of my list. To me it just didn't feel right that the clerk had seen nothing. How could he not see anything, he's got to be lying.

Keeping my eyes fixed on the booth area, I sat and watched. Every so often the clerk would look over at me, sizing me up I thought. My face was not a regular one for him, nor was that of my partner because we were working a different shift from what was our usual. Our normal shift was four-to-twelve but because of the crimes we were assigned to work eight in the morning to four in the afternoon. When we normally went on duty this clerk was on his way home.

He had never seen us and we had never seen him. The same could be said about the station cleaner. Most of the time when the crimes took place it was just before the two got off duty. This was going to be awhile, for it was still early and we had all just started our day.

Sitting and waiting I must have drank at least eight cups of coffee. Every hour my partner and I would switch positions. Him coming up to get air, me going down to sit on the platform. Either way the day dragged on. While sitting on the platform I happened to notice that the cleaner would stop and watch as the passengers left the trains.

Maybe he was keeping an eye out for the guy, maybe he was trying to help. Going about his business of scraping the station he only stopped when a train emptied out. His eyes scanned the platform, looking from side to side he watched the passengers and I watched also.

After a while I noticed that the cleaner was paying more attention to the female passengers than the males. "He's checking out the young ladies," I thought, "He must be looking to pick up a date". That's not unusual, the subway has always been a hunting ground for guys to meet girls and for girls to meet guys. Nothing wrong with that, go for it maybe he'll get lucky.

Somehow though, things didn't seem right. Here I am just sitting on this bench, not making a move to get on a train. Just sitting here checking out the trains and the cleaner isn't worried about me. Far from worrying about me, he didn't pay me the least bit of attention. No, he was watching the trains and the passengers. He made sure that he didn't miss a one.

Three o'clock, the day is moving on and nothing has happened. A whole day wasted sitting on this tiny station. If this guy didn't hit today I would be back here tomorrow and the next day until he did. That was not a pleasant thought. He had to strike and we had to catch him. That's the only way I could keep from being assigned back to this boring station. Sitting for eight hours letting my brain vegetate was not the way I liked spending my day.

After being lost in thought for a few minutes I realized that the cleaner had left the platform. Where did he go? I didn't see him leave. Up the stairs I went, past the booth, over to my partner, "Hey did you see the cleaner?" I asked. "No he didn't come up here," he told me, "Why? What's up?" I told my partner about how the cleaner was acting strangely. How he was checking out the trains and paying close attention to the female passengers. To me this was strange behavior.

With that said, my partner offered some of his own observations. He said that he noticed that the clerk paid little or no attention to the fare beats going into the station, he didn't challenge them at all. The only people that the clerk would pay attention to were female passengers.

He told me whenever a female entered the station carrying a purse, the clerk would tap on the microphone in the booth. The tap could be heard over the speakers on the platform. He also told me of how the cleaner would suddenly appear on the mezzanine after the clerk would tap. The cleaner would check out the female, look towards the clerk and then return to the platform.

I had not paid any attention to the tapping, but now after being made aware of them I thought something was going on. These two were up to something. They had a signal worked out.

If a female entering the station went to the northbound platform the clerk would tap twice. If a female went to the southbound platform the clerk would tap three times. If the cleaner was on the opposite platform he would come up to take a look, then go back downstairs. What were they up to? From the way the pair was acting, we had no choice but to pay closer attention to them.

Three forty-five rolls around. I had come to the realization that I was going to be back at this station tomorrow and the thought of that sucked. Getting prepared to call it a day I got up from the bench and started to head up to my partner. Over the speaker I heard tap, tap, tap. Down the stairway came a female carrying a shoulder bag, she also had a shopping bag in her left hand. Not far behind her was the cleaner.

The two walked past me, with the female stopping halfway down the platform. The cleaner kept going all the way down to the end. Knowing what my partner and I had talked about, I stopped on the stairway out of sight of the female and the cleaner.

Taking out my radio, I told my partner to take up a position on the stairway of the northbound platform. I had the southbound covered. He asked, "What you got?" as he headed to his position. I told my partner that just before the woman came down, I heard the clerk tap on his microphone three times. That meant that a woman was coming to the southbound platform, and right behind her the cleaner had also come down.

I just wanted to watch the cleaner to see what he was doing. It was the right time of day. Their tour was about to end and this is when the purse-snatcher was prone to strike. Watching from the stairs I could see the female, my partner could see the cleaner.

Over the speaker there came a quick tapping loud and fast. This we had not heard all day. Suddenly I heard my partner say over the radio, "Here he comes. The cleaner is running up the platform, what's going on over there?" "Nothing yet," I responded, "Just keep your eyes on him."

As the female turned her head towards the sound of an approaching train the cleaner ran up from behind her. Striking her in the back with his left hand and at the same time ripping away her shoulder bag with his right, he knocked her to the ground and kept on running.

"Oh shit it's him. He just snatched that woman's bag and he's heading straight at me," I thought. Pulling out my shield and gun I bounced down the stairs, "Police, don't move," I yelled. Taking one look at me, the cleaner spun around and began running towards the other end of the station.

I'm in a full sprint trying to catch up to him, past the fallen woman, down the platform we went. Looking over to the northbound side I could see my partner also running at break neck speed down his platform. "Where is he going," I think, "There's no other way out, we got him cornered. When he reaches the end of the platform we got him."

Looking back at me the cleaner now spots my partner on the other platform. As he reaches the end he looks across, there's my partner on the other platform and behind him I'm closing in. Not knowing what to do next, he drops the shoulder bag and makes a wild dash at me. Bracing myself to tackle him I tighten up. As he gets closer to me I have no time to think, just react.

Stepping to the side I stick out my left leg and swing my right arm at the fleeing cleaner. Tripping him while forcing him to the ground he landed with a thud. I jumped on him, cuffs flying out to secure his hands. My partner crosses the tracks and assists me in arresting the cleaner. It's over we got him. The female wasn't hurt and was happy that we caught the robber.

When we brought the cleaner up to the mezzanine in cuffs the clerk's eyes got as wide as a cantaloupe. Seeing the cleaner had been caught, the clerk tried to make a quick exit from the booth. "I don't think so," I said, "Not so fast. I need to talk to you." Standing in front of me with a "oh shit" look on his face the clerk started with, "Look I didn't see anything. I gotta go, get out of my way."

There was no way I was gonna let him leave and I made sure he knew it. Looking him in the eyes I told him why he couldn't leave. I told him how we had figured out the signal between him and the cleaner. I also told him he was under arrest.

My partner and I got credit for the arrest. But the detectives did the final investigation. Turns out that the cleaner and the clerk were long time friends. They had grown up together and were involved in other crimes. The two were arrested in the past for assault, robbery and burglary. They were new employees to the transit system and their background checks had not been completed by the Transit Authority. If it had been, there is no way the two would have been hired.

All of the crimes that the two were arrested for in the past had taken place in the subway. This was there hunting ground. This was the place where they felt at ease going about their hunting. Getting the job working for the Transit Authority made things even better for them. For a while it worked but now they reached the end of the road.

The vision that stays with me about this caper is the look on the cleaner's face after I arrested him. As he stood in front of me looking me over from head to toe, he had the look of a deer caught in headlights on his face. Then he said, "You,

you're a cop? I saw you here all day. I thought you were a pervert or something. You're a fucking cop, ain't that a bitch." The vision of his face as he said this to me was priceless.

CHAPTER 32

▼

THE HOOKER

The want for money can lead many people down the wrong path. I guess the age-old saying that "the love of money is the root of all evil" is true. From some of the visions I observed in my years as a New York City Transit Cop I can truly say that the lust for money was indeed the down fall for many otherwise decent people

Let us take a look at one such person. While patrolling the 179th street station I was making my usual check of the token booth. A check inside the booth revealed a clerk I had not seen before. Introducing myself to him and giving him the once over at the same time, I started my information gathering process.

For me, the need to know something about the people that are working around me is high on my list of priorities. What I learn about the person may not be a lot, but a little is better than nothing. Questions such as: "How long have you worked for the Transit Authority? Where did you work before? Are you going to be the regular person working here?" could give me a good start in getting to know the person.

The clerk didn't have a problem answering my questions, far from it. He was a very chatty person. He told me he was a new employee and that this booth was his first steady assignment. He also stated he had worked as a bank clerk but found that to be a dead-end job. Getting married right after high school he had a wife and two kids.

After talking with a few people that he knew who worked for the Transit Authority, he thought this would be a safe and secure job for him. The benefits were great, the pay was much better than what he was making at the bank and there was plenty of opportunities for advancement.

He went on to tell me that someday he wanted to buy a house on Long Island. How he would be the first in his family to buy a house. His entire family had always rented apartments but he wanted to move past the renting stage and buy a house of his own.

This guy could really talk. I didn't know that once I got him started it would be almost impossible to get him to stop. The information he was giving me was perfect, because this is how I got to know people and with what he was telling me I was getting to know this guy, I thought.

With his mouth moving a mile a minute, he told me that he also wanted to buy a new car. From the time he got his driver's license up until now, he had always driven used cars. Never having the pleasure of being the owner of a brand new car. He wanted to know that feeling.

No one in his family had ever gone to college and he wanted his kids to go. The money he would make from his new job would see to that. Also the Transit Authority had a scholarship program that his kids could participate in, that would almost guarantee them the chance to go to college. This guy just kept on going, he wouldn't stop, on and on he went.

Feeling that I had learned enough for our first encounter I searched for a way to break free from the talkative clerk. With each pause in the conversation I thought, "That's it, I'm out." But no, he would start with another list of the things he hoped to achieve.

Finally after about an hour of listening to this guy I got my out. Over the radio came a call for me. Stopping him in mid-sentence I said, "That's for me, I gotta go. Hold that thought and we'll talk later." Rushing away from the booth I made it look like I had an emergency call. In reality the call was for me to meet the Sergeant, just a check up visit.

The days went past and each time I came across the clerk we had another round of conversations. After getting used to his longwinded stories I knew where to hangout if I got bored on the road. He would always wake me up and keep me alert with the way he talked.

Adding into each statement a sort of question like, "Know what I mean, ain't that something," or the old, "That ever happen to you?" Whatever the question was going to be I had to be ready to answer. I had to listen, so I would know what I was agreeing to or disagreeing with.

The probation for a clerk was six months. He made it through without any problems. His supervisors liked him, the public liked him and I had come to like him. With the personality he possessed it was easy for people like him. He would talk you into liking him. Basically, one would have no choice. He just made you like him, whether you wanted to or not.

The amount of money that any one token booth takes in a day depends on the amount of people that frequents it. 179th street is a busy station. The morning rush is huge. People that live on Long Island or further out in Queens would either take a bus or be driven to the station to continue their commute into the city. Queens is a two fare or three fare zone unless you live close to the subway, but most don't. During the week, Monday through Friday, this station took in a great deal of money.

The money collected during a given tour is placed into a vault located inside the booth. Each clerk before he or she goes off duty must tally up the money, bag it and place it into the safe. Now, when I say safe I'm not talking about a regular safe. Not the type with a combination. No, the booth safes are large steel boxes that have a spinning slot on top.

The bag is placed into the slot and a wheel is spun, dropping the moneybag into the belly of the safe. There is no way for someone to place their hand into the box to pull the bags out. Having the spinning slot so tightly fitted in the box there wasn't anyway an object could be placed into the box to remove the bags, or so it seemed.

For the money to be removed a revenue train had to come. The revenue personnel had to use two sets of keys to unlock the safe from the outside. After unlocking the safe with the keys, a latch had to be pulled from the inside by the clerk at the same time a latch was being pulled on the outside. This made the safe very secure.

Most of the time the Transit Authority was very efficient in emptying the safes once a week, on different days at different times. Without notice the revenue train would show up. The days and times had to be varied so that if anyone was trying to get a read on when the train was going to be at a certain station it would be impossible to do.

This was a good plan and worked well for years. But when things went wrong and the train didn't make a pickup there could be at least two weeks or more between pickups. When a pickup was made on time the safe would never be full for very long, so not even the clerks could get an idea about how much money was in it.

The clerk I had come to know always worked the three-to-eleven shift. He didn't work days because he had to get the kids off to school. His wife worked days so getting the kids out was his job. He didn't work nights because he wanted to be home with his family. The three-to-eleven shift was perfect for him. A little over a year had gone by and the clerk had gotten into a groove working the booth, he had his own system.

While working overtime before the start of my regular shift one day, I again was at 179th street. To my surprise the three-to-eleven clerk was in the booth. "Why was he here?" I had to know. Telling me that he also was on overtime, he went on to say that his paycheck just wasn't enough anymore. He needed to work overtime to make ends meet. Everything in the city had gone up in price and he was feeling the heat. "A man's gotta do what a man's gotta do," he would say.

My answer was a resounding, "I know what you mean I'm in the same boat. The more you make the more you spend, believe me I know how you feel." Overtime was nothing new for me, I took as much as I could get. So his telling me that he was doing the same was fine with me, get all you can.

During the next few weeks, my overtime took me from before the tour to after the tour. No matter which tour I worked I would see the friendly clerk. We were both racking up, fattening up the paychecks while also giving half to Uncle Sam. The clerk and I talked about our upcoming vacations. Where we wanted to go, what we wanted to do.

With all the overtime we were clocking, affording to go away and still have money in the bank was going to be easy. I would be going first and about the time my vacation was ending the clerk would be starting his.

Well vacation came and went so fast that when I got back to work it felt like I had never left. My first day back I didn't expect to see the friendly clerk in the booth and true to my thinking he wasn't there. I started in on the relief clerk with my standard question and answer session.

She told me that she was going to be in that booth for two weeks while the regular clerk was on vacation. This I knew but I wasn't letting on, for I was in my information-gathering mode. Didn't get much though, she had an attitude with cops. To each their own.

Sometime during the first week of the regular clerk's vacation the revenue train came to make their pickup. The bags did not add up, there was a shortage. A shortage was putting it nicely. Inside the safe were only five bags of money. It should have contained about forty-two bags because for some reason the past two weeks pickups were not made.

Why were there only five bags of money in the safe? Had there been a pickup by another revenue train and this crew didn't know? Calling into their headquarters the answer came back fast, "No." No one had made a pickup, something was wrong.

This started the investigation. The booth was crawling with detectives. The Transit Authority was doing an audit. Every penny was being accounted for. A closer inspection of the moneybags that were still remaining in the safe revealed something strange. Embedded in the bags were fishing hooks. Fishing hooks with broken lines attached to them. What was going on here, why would fishing hooks be in the safe?

The answer was obvious, someone had pulled the bags out of the safe using the fishing hooks and line. The question now was, who and when. Every clerk who had worked that booth for the past two weeks was being questioned. Everyone that had access to the booth was brought in, that is except the regular guy who was on vacation. After completing their list of suspects except for one, the detectives waited for the regular clerk to return, for now the investigation was at a standstill.

The day came that the regular clerk was to return and the detectives were ready for him. Poised outside the booth they waited for him to show up for work. They waited and waited and waited. No clerk, the day tour clerk was still in the booth. Questioning the day tour clerk as to why he was still there, the detectives were informed that he was told the regular clerk was supposed to be coming and should be on his way. Three hours had gone by and still no sign of the regular clerk. Feeling that something was wrong, the detectives decided to pay the clerk a visit at his home.

Arriving at the address of the clerk, the detectives were taken back for a second. Looking at each other with questioning expressions on their faces the two spoke the same words at the same time, "This is the correct address right? This is what they gave us, right?" Taking a look through their paperwork proved the address was correct, but something was wrong. Maybe they were at the right address but in the wrong borough.

A call to verify the address gave them the same results. They were in the right place. This was the correct address. Staring out the windows of their patrol car the two could only shake their heads and wonder how? How could someone give an address to a vacant lot as their residence? Work for the city for over a year and not have it checked out, this stumped them. Now they knew for sure who they were looking for. All they had to do was gather more information from the Transit Authority on this guy and start their search.

Well, they got the information they wanted from the Transit Authority: Background information, mother and father names, name of relatives, also the schools that he attended. They even got his social security number but none of it helped. Why you may ask? Because the entire identity of the friendly clerk was false, his social security number belonged to a man who died many years before and his so-called family did not exist.

A check of the fingerprints obtained from the booth did help. The friendly clerk turned out to be a career criminal who served time in prison for bank robbery and forgery. He had been released two years earlier and disappeared at the same time the friendly clerk appeared. Now he was gone again, this time along with many bags of money.

The Transit Authority never released the exact amount of money, but it's said to be quite a bit. This event led the city and the Transit Authority to change the way background checks were done on new employees. No longer would the little things like name, address and social security be checked at the end of probation, these checks would be done in the beginning. The money and the friendly clerk were never seen again.

The expressions on the faces of the transit supervisors was something to be seen, boy they looked stupid. Whenever this case comes up, they still get the same stupid look on their faces. The vision of their faces still makes me laugh.

CHAPTER 33

▼

MONEY, MONEY, MONEY

Greed is something that can be found in the most trusted person, when placed in the right situation. The want for money can be over powering even if the person is making a good living, has no pressure from being late with bills and can afford just about whatever he or she wants.

When placed in a situation where temptation can run amuck, some will give into that temptation. The money that is collected by the Transit Authority on any given day is astounding. At the time the cost of each ride was a dollar and seventy-five cents, and most riders pay twice, one fare to go and another fare to come back. With the amount of riders that take the subway and buses each day the figures are through the roof.

The people hired to collect and count the vast amount of money must be very trustworthy. Background checks must be done as long as the employee holds one of those positions. Everything must be checked and rechecked. There cannot be any doubt as to the character of the person. Getting the position as a revenue agent can take a long time.

The persons hired to do this job usually come from inside the Transit Authority. They are present employees that have been working for the Transit Authority for sometime and have an impeccable work record. The person must be clean as a whistle. He or she must have proven they can indeed be trusted to handle such a great amount of money.

Being selected for the position of revenue collector is a promotion for the ones that are chosen. Most of the ones selected come from working as a token booth clerk or a station cleaner. The benefits are the same but the pay is raised quite a bit.

Some of the revenue collectors ride the money train. A great number of people selected as Revenue Protection Agents when given a choice of being a counter or collector choose to ride the train because along with this position comes the opportunity to carry a gun.

The gun is the final draw. Feeling like a cop but not having the responsibility of a cop was a high to them. Others didn't want the gun, they did not want the responsibility that came with it. For them, being a counter and working inside a secure building was fine. What could happen to someone working in the money room, the vault of the Transit Authority?

If you think Fort Knox is locked down tighter than the rusted lid of a molasses jar, the Transit vault would have been thought of as that rusted molasses jar sealed inside of cement. This place was inviolable no one got in or out without being searched, scanned and searched again. Located on the twelfth floor of the Transit building, the vault took up half the floor. Just getting to the twelfth floor was a challenge in its self.

After boarding the elevator a special key had to be placed into a slot for the elevator to move past the eleventh floor. Once the elevator reached the vault floor, before the doors would be opened, the identity of each and every person inside had to be verified by the revenue protection agent stationed outside the doors.

Having been passed by this agent the person or persons traveling to the vault would then proceed down a long hallway where they were again met by another agent sitting outside a large steel door with cameras affixed to them to record the action outside.

After making it pass this agent, the door would open and once you stepped inside it would close. Another hallway was ahead. One would proceed down to the end and be met by another agent sitting outside of another steel door with cameras. Identity checked again.

With entry granted, stepping though this door revealed another hallway and at the end of it was yet another agent sitting outside of steel barred doors, beyond them was the vault. The room was huge. It contained stacks and stacks of bags filled with money.

Working in the vault were the counters, clad in jumpsuit type uniforms that didn't have pockets. The counters went about their job of opening and counting the monies that had been collected. There wasn't much talking. Everyone was focused on the money, counting, counting, and counting. Eight hours a day counting money. Lose track and they would have to start over again, that wasn't a good thing.

Looking around the vault there were three windows, all of which had their panes replaced with bullet resistant glass. The glass was then coated with a film that would let the workers see out but not let anyone see into the room. Even though this was the twelfth floor, the windows were also sealed shut. There was no way to open them besides breaking them. Once inside the vault for their shift, the workers were not allowed out until it was time to leave for the day.

Located in the rear of the vault was the employee lounge where lunch and breaks were taken. Not much was in the room: Only a large table, a few chairs, microwave oven, refrigerator, and stove. Above the stove was a fan vent to suck out any smoke and heat.

Working in the vault had to be boring. No radio, no television, nothing to distract the counters from the money. Day in and day out just counting money, and what a great deal of money it was. Some have been known to say that the vault contained so much money that it was impossible to count it all. Not even the Transit Authority knew exactly how much money was in the vault.

The rumor was that there was money that had been collected two or three years in the past that had not been counted. The bags kept on coming faster than the counters could count. Three times a day, everyday, the bags were being dropped off, the cycle never ended.

Seeing all this money had to be tempting to some, with so much of it how would the Transit Authority miss a few bags? Just a couple of bags and no one would know. But how would the bags be removed without being spotted? That was the problem.

There wasn't any way possible to get a penny out of the room and a bag was out of the question. Like I said before, the vault was on complete lock down. Everything and everyone that went in or out was inspected, re-inspected and inspected again. The removal of unauthorized money could not be done without the person being caught.

Working the vault took its toll on most of the employees that accepted the job. The turnover rate was high. Most only lasted five years locked inside the vault before they had to be reassigned. That is except one. There was this one guy who worked inside the vault for fifteen years. He worked for the Transit Authority for over thirty years and was the perfect employee. Good sick record, no complaints and happy in what he was doing, he was well liked and trusted by all.

Over the years he had seen employees come and go. Some just couldn't take being locked inside a room all day. Those employees, fed up with all the counting requested to be removed from the vault. There were also those that were thought to be scheming on various ways to steal, even though they hadn't taken any money, they had to be removed.

Yeah, the employees came and went but this guy stayed. Year after year he stayed, counting away doing his time and not complaining. Not giving anyone a reason to raise an eyebrow. Over the years of working in the poorly lit vault, the bad lighting took its toll on the old-timer. With his eyesight getting worse he found it harder and harder to focus on the counting. Having to take more frequent breaks to clear his eyes, he was now starting to have problems with his supervisors. The headaches started coming and nothing he did stopped them for very long.

With his work now being affected at an increasing rate, his supervisors looked to have him removed from the vault. With all his years of service in the vault it was not easy to have him removed. He had no formal complaints and even though his speed had slowed he was still keeping up with the counts of others. But how long would he be able to keep up? He knew deep down inside his days were numbered. The job that he loved would soon be taken away from him. Not being able to have him removed from the vault, his supervisor turned to the task of trying to make him leave on his own free will.

Every movement that the old-timer made was watched. His breaks were now being timed, ten minutes only, not a second longer. Lunch was thirty minutes and that's all. He was given no extra time. With the supervisor breathing down his neck day after day he started to feel resentment towards his job.

How could he be treated this way after so many years? Not once over his career had he given them a reason to think that he wasn't doing his job. Not once had he given them a problem. He did everything that was asked of him and more. How could they now treat him as if he was obsolete, like a broken piece of furniture to be tossed away?

No, he wasn't going to be treated this way, not after all his time of working and slaving away for them. Filing a complaint of harassment with the union against his supervisor got him nowhere. In fact it only made things worse because now there would be retaliation. The supervisor struck back by removing him from his counting station and assigning him to stacking and cleaning duties. No longer would he be a counter, he was just a high paid cleaner.

Complaining to the union about the way he was being treated didn't help. He was told that the supervisor could assign him to whatever task had to be done in the vault. He was being paid to work the vault and counting was only part of what went on inside. If he didn't like his new assignment he would have to leave the vault and work elsewhere.

During the next couple of months he just went along with every dirty job the supervisor threw at him. He didn't complain. He said nothing while going about his tasks. Approaching the supervisor one day, the old-timer told him that he wanted to put the past issues to rest. He wanted to move on and forget about what had taken place between the two.

Telling of how he had such a long and happy time working in the vault he now felt that maybe the supervisor was correct in removing him from his counting duties, seeing how bad his eyesight had become. Since he was no longer counting the headaches had stopped, he felt much better. Maybe it was time for him to move on?

He had not been able to come to grips with the fact that it was time for him to go. It took his supervisor removing him from his position as a counter to show him the light. He went on thanking the supervisor, adding that he had filed for retirement. He only had a week to work. He just wanted to clear the air before leaving, no hard feelings.

Accepting the apology of the old-timer and offering his own gesture of good will the two got along well for the next week. The supervisor even gave the old-timer a farewell party along with a gift for all his years of service and wished him well as his last day had come.

Not too long after the old-timer retired, a small fire broke out in the vault. The fire caused no damage because it was mostly smoke. The smoke had built up in the vent fan of the stove. Something was stuck in the vent blocking the free movement of air. After the smoke cleared the vent was inspected by the fire department to determine what was blocking it. No one really knew where the vent let out. All they knew was that it was a vent and most likely ran straight outside behind the stove.

Wrong, the vent ran the entire length of the building, from the twelfth floor to the basement. Where it was then routed outside. Tracing the vent down its course, looking for the blockage the firemen came upon a fantastic sight.

There in the basement at the end of the vents run was a trap door, a clean out opening. When the door was opened and a pry bar inserted, out fell empty moneybags. The bags rolled out of the vent onto the floor. How did they get in the vent, who put them there, when were the bags placed in the vent?

An audit of the vault revealed that the bags had been placed in the vent over years. The tags on some of the bags went back more than fifteen years. Now the question focused on whom? The basement is where the employees that worked the vault parked their cars. Each spot was numbered and assigned to an employee.

The employee that occupied the spot next to the vent was the old-timer who just retired. He had that spot all his years working in the vault. After his retirement the old-timer left the country. Word was that he moved to South America, no one really knew, because he was never seen or heard from again.

The Transit Authority never released a set figure on how much money was missing and I guess they never will. After being raked over the coals, the people in charge of the revenue department were let go and the department reorganized.

The entire unit was remodeled, even the break room. The stove was removed and the vent sealed. When asked about the incident at public hearings, a spokesman for the Transit Authority would give a blank expression and state, "No comment." I guess the vision of all that money walking away left him speechless.

CHAPTER 34

▼

RAKING IN THE DOUGH

Now I don't want to give you the impression that stealing from the Transit Authority is easy. It's not and everyone that does steal doesn't get away with it. Quite the opposite, the majority of the people who steal from the Transit system are caught. Whatever their reasons, some just think they have the master plan. They believe they can take whatever they want and no one will ever catch them.

This is what one token clerk thought. She worked for the city for ten years, taking the abuse of the public and her supervisors. Her pay was good and there wasn't anything that she needed or wanted that she could not buy. After all her years of taking in so much money, she started to wonder how it would feel if she got to keep it all instead of turning it over to the city.

Yeah, she was getting paid but she wanted more. The city was raking tons of money in each day and what they were paying her wasn't enough. With such large sums of money coming in, how would they miss a few dollars? The more she thought about it the more she convinced herself that she would be able to steal and not get caught.

As she toiled through each day she racked her brain on just how to get away with taking the money and not being caught. For every plan she came up with, she weighed the negative and the positive. Nothing that came to her would work, each plan led to her being caught.

There had to be a foolproof plan. All she had to do was keep thinking until she thought of the right idea. Getting the plan correct was the only thing that she could think about. When she was not working, most of her day was spent reading or watching stories about past robberies that had been pulled off successfully.

When she first came up with the idea of stealing, it made her nervous just thinking about doing it. Now she wasn't nervous, she was determined to make the money hers. Plan after plan came to her, none were right. Going to jail was out of the question.

No way was she going to jail and at the least she wasn't about to lose her job if she was suspected of taking the money but could not be proven guilty. No, her plan had to be perfect, get the money and keep her job also. That was the way she wanted things to go.

One day while going about her duties, over the booth intercom came an announcement about a booth robbery in the Bronx. The announcement didn't give much detail but it gave enough to spark an idea in her. The next day she gathered all the newspapers that carried stories about the booth robbery.

Reading and studying the details of the robbery was fascinating to her. Talking with other clerks while picking their brains for any piece of inside information they had, she began to put together her plan. From what she came up with, her plan was simple. So simple in fact, she wondered why it took her so long to come up with it. The plan was so good that all of the aspects that she wanted fell into place without a hitch.

Not only would she get the money but she would be the victim also. Being the victim no one would suspect her. She would most likely be given some time off to recover from such a horrifying event before returning back to work.

Getting away with the money, having time off and retaining her job this was the perfect plan, this was it. Not wanting to rush into her plan, the clerk ran it through her mind for a few weeks to make sure that it was indeed perfect. After all her thinking was completed she was ready to move forward. Picking the correct day to pull it off was all she had to do next.

The Christmas shopping season was approaching and the subways were filling up more and more each day with shoppers. More riders meant more money being taken in. The bags being dropped into the safe at the end of their tours by the clerks had doubled. Money was just pouring in. If she was going to go through with her plan this was the right time. With the Christmas season came added riders and more money for the clerks. For me it brought about something different.

For the police department when this time of year rolls around it means stepping up patrols and assigning officers to just one station for twelve hours. This made for a very long day, walking around the same station for twelve hours, seeing the same people come and go. When assigned to a holiday post the officer is to remain as visible as possible, let the people see you. Get the word out that there is a cop patrolling the station. This way if any one is thinking about committing a crime they will think twice.

I spent most of my time just standing in the middle of the mezzanine. I had to be seen by anyone entering or exiting the station. Nothing was going to happen on my station, not if I had anything to say about it.

Taking a break from the mezzanine, I would walk the platforms every once in awhile. Can't forget about them, what if someone came in on a train and was setting up for a crime on the platform. If they didn't see me down there, they wouldn't hesitate to strike. A sweep of the platforms and then back to the mezzanine, that's how my day went.

Whenever I did take a walk from the mezzanine I made sure to vary my time. This way if someone was trying to clock me it would be impossible. I had no idea of when I would take a walk around, but I knew it wouldn't be at the same time as the previous one.

While standing on the mezzanine, I noticed the clerk was staring at me whenever there wasn't a person at the booth, she was watching me. I thought maybe she wanted something from upstairs or maybe she needed to use the toilet. Over to the booth I went, "Everything alright? You need anything?" I asked.

She was polite answering, "No, I was just wondering why you were here all day? You have been here as long as I have." Not wanting to reveal my assignment to her I just stated, "Since there were so many people at this station, I felt that I should spend more time here," adding, "Is that a problem with you?"

Most clerks would be happy to have a cop on their station all day. Why was she worrying about me? What I was doing should not bother her. My being here should make her day easier. Not thinking much about what the clerk said I returned to my position.

Over the radio came a report of a booth robbery followed by a description of the perpetrator. The booth robbery took place in my working area but across town from where I was. Fleeing in a car, the robber made a clean getaway. I copied down the information and gave another check of my station. Nothing like that was going to happen here, not on my watch.

Because this was an extended tour for me, my meal period was set later than normal. I had to work seven hours before I got to eat. This meant that my meal would start about the time that I would normally be leaving to head back to the command for the change of tour.

Mealtime was approaching and I was ready for it. But before I went I gave the station one final look, everything was fine. Being that it was only an hour after the booth robbery took place, I wanted to make sure that my station was tight before I left. Finding everything ok, I proceeded to head upstairs in search of food. The restaurant that I planned to get my lunch from was located on the rear of the station so that's the way I went out. Not having to walk past the booth, the clerk nor the passengers would see me leave.

Having purchased my food, I returned to the station the same way I left. Using my keys I entered the station at the rear. My lunch would be enjoyed while I sat in the cleaners break room. Out of sight of the public away from the crush of people swarming around. I made my way into the room unseen again by the clerk.

The food wasn't the best but it was better than nothing, at least I had something in my stomach and was finally sitting down. About halfway through my meal period I looked at my watch, the thought that if not for the extended tour I would be heading back by now griped me. But now I still had some time to go, so I enjoyed the rest of my quiet time and got set to finish out the tour.

Leaning back in my seat to relax, my peace was interrupted by a call coming over the radio, "All units be advised we have a report of a booth robbery in progress, male armed with a gun." Sitting up in my chair I listened closely waiting for the station to be named.

Then to my shock the operator states that the robbery is taking place on my station. Grabbing my hat and stick I ran out onto the mezzanine yelling into the radio telling the operator that I am on the station and preceding towards the booth. As I ran to the booth again I heard the radio, the operator is stating that the report is coming from the clerk.

Gun in hand now I am getting closer to the booth, but something looks wrong. There are a lot of people on the mezzanine no one is acting like anything is going on. The people are just watching me run towards the booth, no one is saying anything. Slowing my pace I take a good look at the booth, the clerk is still selling tokens. There are people on line waiting and no fuss is being made.

As I arrive at the booth the clerk looks up, her eyes get wide as she sees me. Noticing that I have my gun out, the people who were on line started moving away. "What's going on?" I asked the clerk, "Where did he go? What did he look like? Are you alright?"

Stunned for a moment, all of a sudden she starts to cry and scream, "He robbed me. I went to clear out my turnstiles and when I was coming back to the booth he robbed me!" She went on to give me a full description of what the guy looked like and also stated that he fled to the street.

After notifying Central of what I had learned, I started to set up a crime scene. While doing this, I realized the clerk had calmed down a great deal. Not only calmed down but was acting as if nothing had taken place. Maybe she was in shock. Maybe this is how she was dealing with what she had just gone through?

Then out of the blue it hit me. The radio said the robbery was in progress when the broadcast was made. It had taken me no longer than fifteen seconds to reach the booth after I heard the call. Why had I not seen the guy flee? Why, if the clerk was being robbed had the passengers not reacted to the robbery? Someone would have said something? Why was the clerk still sitting and selling tokens when I got to the booth? Something was definitely wrong.

I questioned the clerk as to why she was not upset when I first got to the booth. Why did everything look so normal? Her response was, "Where did you come from? How did you get here so fast? I thought you left!" Turning my head towards the clerk I said in a questioning tone, "What? What do you mean how did I get here so fast? I never left I've been here all along!" Frowning her face she stated, "Aren't you supposed to be off duty now? Why are you still here? What do you mean you never left, I didn't see you!"

Now I knew something was definitely wrong with this situation. I told the clerk to stay in the booth while I went out to speak with some of the people that were still hanging around. While questioning the people one thing stuck out, all of them I questioned gave basically the same story.

They said while waiting to buy tokens or just waiting for the train, they observed the clerk pickup the phone and make a call. Right after she hung up the next thing they saw was me rushing towards the booth. When asked if they had seen anyone else in the booth with the clerk they all answered no. Nothing out of the norm had taken place at the booth until I had gotten there. That's when all the action started.

As the troops landed on the station and the situation calmed down, I spoke to the detective that was interviewing the clerk. Telling him what I saw and the answers I received from the passengers about what they saw, he looked at me and smiled. "How long did it take you to get to the booth," he asked me. "About fifteen seconds," I stated. "That's what I thought you said," he stated to me through his smiling lips

After talking to the clerk for another few minutes, the detective was ready to take her back to the command to look at pictures and complete his report. Getting ready to leave, the clerk picked up her shoulder bag and started to head out the door. "I'll carry that for you," the detective said while reaching for her shoulder bag. While holding onto the shoulder bag the detective glanced over to me and winked but said nothing.

After reaching the command we headed into the detectives office, "Hey guy, could you hold this for a minute?" the detective said to me while he placed the shoulder bag into my hand. As the bag settled into my grip I noticed that it was very heavy. "What's she got in this thing?" I thought, "Bricks." I sat the bag down on a desk in the detective's office and started to leave but was stopped and asked to stay.

Directing the clerk to have a seat, the detective started with more questions to the clerk. Looking up from his desk, the detective again winked at me. He than sat back in his chair and coldly asked the clerk, "You want to stick to your story or do you want to tell me the truth now? I know you weren't robbed and I'm letting you know it, so if you want to come clean, now is the time to do so!"

I'm standing in the corner watching all this thinking, "What's he up to?" When suddenly the clerk bows her head and again starts to cry. With her entire body shaking she blurted out, "I'm sorry." Crying like a baby the clerk sat there, shaking and pleading.

"Where's the money," the detective asked, "Can I look in your bag?" Shaking her head while answering yes, the clerk gave permission for the detective to look into her shoulder bag. From the shoulder bag the detective removed several bags of money along with a couple of boxes of tokens and sat them on the desk. "Now you want to tell me what happened," the detective asked the clerk.

As the crying clerk started to tell of her plan, I looked at her and shook my head. "That stupid bitch," I thought to myself as I left the room. How the hell did she think she was going to get away with stealing all that money? Damn, she's stupid. In the detectives office she laid out her entire plan and pleaded for mercy.

After she completed giving her statement the detective called me back to the office. He told me what she said to him. How she planned everything, everything that is, except me getting to the booth so quickly. She thought I was on my way back to the command for the change of tour and that it should have taken longer for the cops to arrive. I had gotten there too fast and ruined everything. As I left the detectives office, the vision of the clerk sitting there crying was pitiful.

CHAPTER 35

▼

GIVE ME THE MONEY

Police officers make good money, not as much as they should, but still they make good money. With overtime an officer can double his or her pay, which then makes the pay great. However, working the amount of overtime needed to achieve this can take its toll on an officer. The long hours out on patrol, the sore feet from all the walking and standing not to mention the time away from one's family, all of these things can lead to different or adverse effects on anyone.

After working long hours each day for a number of years, one would have to think there has to be a better way of obtaining the extra money needed to live the lifestyle they have become accustomed to. Keep working the overtime that is wearing one's body and mind down or come up with an idea that will take the pressure off while still bringing in the money needed. One way is to open a small business that will generate the income but not over burden the person.

There was one officer I knew who wanted to do just that. He wanted to start a business that would as he put it, "Pay the bills, clothe the kids and keep the wife fat." Tired of working long hours on the road, he searched for an idea that would free him from the grip of the overtime monster. The need for extra money was not great, but the want was.

Being accustomed to wearing the best clothing and driving a new car every three years had become a habit to him and his wife. She was a fashion plate and he wasn't far behind her. Whatever the newest style was they had it, along with the latest model cars. Keeping their kids out of the public school system was also of upper most importance. With the goal of getting into a renowned college, it was only private schools for them. They did not want their kids to be blue-collar workers. Doctor, lawyer, or politician is what the plan was for the kids, nothing shorter.

To reach these goals and still live well was what the officer wanted and he was going to reach his goals at any cost. Year after year he schemed of ways to put an end to relying on overtime. He played the lotto and also the illegal numbers. Any shot at hitting it big was worth a try. Sometimes he won but never big enough to fill his wants. He always wanted more.

One day while attending a softball game between our command and another, the officer paid more attention to the guy selling hot dogs than the game. Watching closely as the vendor sold his wares, noting how many people lined up to buy sodas and hotdogs, an idea was forming in the officer's mind.

Leaving his seat, he made his way over to the vendor and began collecting information about owning and operating a hotdog cart. The vendor was very forth coming in relating just what it took to get started and how to go about picking out and setting up in the right locations. Overhead was not that much. The cost of operating the business depended on what you were going to stock. Hot dogs were cheap, the buns were cheaper, and everything that was sold from the cart gave a higher return then what was paid for them.

This seemed to be the perfect thing. Just what he was looking for. Buy a cart, stock it well. Find a good location and he would be on his way. The most expensive part would be the license to sell food.

After weeks of research, the officer decided this was what he wanted to do. Thinking that he could work the cart after he completed his tour of duty, picking and choosing where to set up and how long to work a given area was up to him. The longer he worked, the more he would make and the more he made the more he could spend.

Charging head strong into the hotdog business he bought his first cart and license. To get the business started he took out a personal loan with the idea that once he got rolling with the hotdogs, he would pay off the loan in no time. To make the most out of his new adventure he changed from working the four-to-twelve tour to the overnight tour.

With the change, he could spend his days selling the hotdogs and shut down with enough time left over to rest up before returning to patrol. Working the cart during the day he was making good money. He chose a spot not far from a hospital and school, located between the two there was a busy subway station. With the high volume of foot traffic, his business was off to a good start.

Even with the increase in the flow of money that was coming in, he felt he could do better. Thinking back to when he first got the idea to open the cart something hit him. He had been working the cart mostly Monday through Friday. Hitting the working and school crowds he was making money but more could be made if he were to work the different parks of the city on the weekends.

During the spring and summer months the parks were always overflowing with people. Sporting events drew large crowds. Mothers with their kids and even the people that were just relaxing would give his cart a huge boost. Not everyone that ventured into the parks packed their lunch. Even if they did, most would not pass up the chance to down a hotdog.

The officer put in a request to have his days off changed to steady Saturday and Sunday, the request was granted. Now he was set. Monday to Friday work the school, hospital and subway crowd. Restocking on the weekends he would work the parks. Perfect. His plan was working like a charm. The money was pouring in with him selling out his complete supply of hotdogs before night fell. With the business doing so well he felt that it was time to expand. If one cart brought in so much money having two or three would put him on easy street.

Taking out another loan he bought two other carts and staffed them with people he knew from the streets. When hiring someone to work for you, one must be sure that the person can be trusted especially when handling money is involved. Each cart was making a profit and the officer was on cloud nine. This is what he had envisioned, less work, more money. Life was great, it couldn't get any better but it could get worse.

As the months went along there came a time when he noticed that the profits from his two other carts had been falling off. Each week the profits that were coming in from the other two carts got smaller, something was wrong. Why was the cart he worked still making the big money and the others weren't? How can this be?

The carts were being placed in the same locations and the flow of people had not decreased. So what's happening to the money? Having decided that there was only one reason the carts were short, he began watching his employees more intensely. They had to be pocketing and he knew it. All he had to do was catch them.

Downing his cart and setting up watch on the other two he saw how they were stealing from him. For every two hotdogs that were sold, the employees would pocket half the money. They were getting fat off of him and he had caught them.

Their stealing would have been difficult to catch without spying on them and observing them pocketing the money, because no leftover hotdogs were counted.

The unsold hotdogs were disposed of and the exact amount that was sold could not be tracked. Confronting the two thieves the officer fired them both. Now he was back down to just the one cart.

Trying his best to fill the spots of the two fired employees he found no takers. No one wanted to stand behind a hotdog cart all day making what he was paying. If they did, they also wanted a cut from the sales. The officer was not about to give them that. With his profits down to where he started, the officer began having problems paying the bills. When he had just the one cart everything was fine but with having to pay the loan for three carts while only one was working was eating away all profits, there were none.

Having to make up the difference from his paycheck was hitting him hard. He was in worse shape now than when he started. With the bills mounting up and his wife on his back everything was falling apart. Going back to working overtime while putting in extra hours at the hotdog cart and still not making enough money to keep the creditors off his back was starting to weigh heavy on the officer.

Throwing himself into working as much overtime as he could get, he became known as the Code 99 master. Code 99 was what the department called the overtime. Blood money is what the officers called it. There was so much overtime. Four hours before the regular tour, four hours after and having to work your first day off, it never stopped. More time was spent at the command than at home, and some of the officers couldn't have been happier.

The indebted officer seemed to never leave the command he was always there. When I came in he was on patrol, when I left he was on patrol. He was a working machine. Month after month went by and the officer kept up his pace of working.

One day on my way into work, I noticed the officer's car. His car was hard to miss. It was a pink Cadillac with a white roof. It stood out and there was no other like it. What got my attention was the license plate, "Code 99" it read in bold black letters. After reading the plate I laughed to myself. If one didn't know whose car it was before, there was no mistaking who owned it now.

Out on patrol I ran into the officer and couldn't help but comment on his new plate. He just smiled and said, "Well 99 paid for it, so I might as well give it the credit due." Looking at the officer I noticed that he had lost a lot of weight, his hair had gotten gray, he just looked worn.

Working all that overtime and the hotdog cart was doing him in. "You gotta slow down," I told him, "You're not looking too good, give the overtime a break." As he walked away from me he stated, "A man's gotta do what a man's gotta do." That was the last I saw of the officer for a while, he did his thing and I did mine.

Overtime for police officers come and go, but Code 99 had lasted longer than any of the others. But all good things must come to an end and so did Code 99. With the overtime gone, life was getting back to normal, go in at the regular time and go home at the regular time. Getting back to a somewhat normal life was great. Then it happened, a rash of booth robberies, two or three a day. Each day on different stations throughout the command a booth was being robbed.

There was only one perpetrator. He had a gun but never shot anyone. He would always strike when the clerks were about to change tours, for most booths this was at the same time that the officers changed tours. After robbing the booth the male would run up to the street to make his getaway.

It was assumed that he was using a car. With so many booths being robbed the department flooded the area with officers from different commands throughout the city. Each station in my command was on lock down. Putting an end to the robberies and catching the perpetrator was all that mattered.

The robberies were only happening in my command's area on the day or the four-to-twelve tours, none on the overnight shift. From the way the robberies were taking place it was thought that the guy committing them knew the system.

Maybe he was an ex-employee? Maybe he was a present employee? No one knew but he did know a lot about the system. Another two weeks had passed and the robberies still continued. More cops were brought in to tighten the trap. Something had to give, this guy had to be caught.

While shuffling around a station one day I heard my radio broadcast a booth robbery. The guy struck again but this time there were cops staking out the station and they were on his tail. Listening to my radio I was shocked at what I heard next. The cops in pursuit of the robber were chasing a pink Cadillac with a white roof. Its license plate read "Code 99." Not believing what I heard, I listened again to the description of the car being chased. It was true. The car was that of the "Overtime King." He was the booth robber.

Ending the chase with the crash of his Cadillac, the officer that had gone bad was arrested. As he was led into the command he held his head down and said nothing. Other officers gathered around him to get a look at the bad seed, me included.

Led into the detective's office, the officer began to talk. He told of the bills that wouldn't go away. He told of the need and want for a better life for his wife and kids. He told of the pressure that was on him to provide for them and to make sure they never wanted for anything.

It was his job to better the family and keep it stable. With the failure of his hotdog carts and the end of Code 99 overtime there was no way he could keep up with the bills. So he did what he had to do. For him that was robbing token booths.

The sad sight of the officer being led out the command on his way to Central Booking through the lines of reporters with cameras flashing is still imprinted in my mind. This vision I still remember and will never forget.

CHAPTER 36

▼

WHO A COP? YOU A COP?

Robbing token booths is nothing new. As long as there have been token booths they have been robbed. Either by employees or from others that feel the booths are easy targets. The ways in which booths have been robbed are as vast as the different varieties of people that inhabit the earth. The robberies can range from violent to nonviolent. Most of the robberies happen at the end of a gun. Sneak thieves committed the others.

One of the most fascinating groups of robberies that I came across during my years was the ones committed by a team that were dubbed the salt and pepper bandits. Committing the robberies at different times and in different parts of the city the duo had struck five times. Each robbery was a success for the team, no one was hurt, all the money and tokens they could carry was taken and their getaway was clean.

Trying to set a pattern for the bandits was not easy, they moved around the city striking at will. There weren't a set number of days between each hit. The stations being robbed were spread out over a large area. A robbery could happen in the early morning hours one day the next would be late at night or afternoon. Monday through Friday, Saturday or Sunday, the day did not matter. Whenever the team felt like doing another job they would. The upper hand was theirs and they knew it.

Covering every station in the system around the clock was impossible for the police force. At the time of this robbery spree, the city had been in a hiring freeze for some years. With the police force not at full strength and getting smaller every month with the amount of officers retiring, out injured or sick, it seemed like the team of bandits could go on committing their crimes for as long as they wanted to.

With the city hurting for officers, picking and choosing which stations to cover was like a lottery. The only stations that were guaranteed to have an officer on them were the main ones. All terminals were covered along with large transfer stations, the rest were up for grab.

As the weeks went along, the two robbers kept about their business of robbing at will. There were no patterns that the two stuck with. There were no clues as to the identity of the pair but there was one piece of information that was known by the detectives but not by the officers on patrol. That piece of information was that the robbers wore a police uniform.

That's right, these guys were committing robberies while dressed in a full police officer's uniform. From the hat to the shoes they had it all, the entire uniform and they were using it to their advantage. Information like that would be very important to the officers out on patrol each day, that is if we had the information.

From the start of the robberies, the detectives and the higher ups in the department knew about the uniform but refused to release this information to the police officers. No, they chose to hold onto this vital piece of information until they could have each officer's photo reviewed by the clerks that had been robbed.

The process of gathering and showing the officer's photos was going to take a very long time. Even though the city was short on officers, there were over twenty thousand officers working. In the city there are three main policing agencies, there are the Transit Police, the Housing Police and of course the Street Cops.

Gathering information from each branch was not easy because none of the three worked together often. Each department had their own way of doing things and refused to compromise their ways.

The worst of the lot was the Street Cops. They felt as if they owned the city. Transit and Housing were just something that had to be dealt with, not listened to or worked with. When the request for the photos of the officers went out to each agency the response was slow.

With the different departments fighting with each other as to who should handle the case, the robbers were left to do what they did best. As the weeks of in house fighting between the different police agencies continued the robberies went on. During all of this the officers out on patrol each day still had no knowledge of the bandits wearing an officer's uniform.

Going out on patrol each day with what I thought was the correct description of the bandits, I would burn it into my mind. The description wasn't much, male black, male white, both about six feet tall, weighing one hundred and fifty to one hundred and eighty pounds each, both between the ages of twenty-five to thirty-five years. That's it, that's all we had to go on.

Long after the two started their crime spree, I began to notice a difference in the way I was being greeted by the clerks. Usually a clerk would be happy to see a cop on their station and would often engage in conversation with the officer. If the weather were cold or overly hot, most clerks would offer to let an officer inside the booth to either warm up or cool off.

Things had began to change, the clerks that I would normally spend some time talking with were giving me the cold shoulder, not talking much if at all. With the weather freezing outside there weren't any offers made by the clerks to share the warmth of the booth.

There was something wrong but I didn't know what. The clerks weren't talking and I couldn't figure out what was going on. I thought that for every clerk to be acting this way they must be worried about the robberies. But why act like this towards the cops, I was there to protect them. To save them from being robbed. Why was I being treated this way?

Unable to get anything out of the clerks I just went on with my patrol, what else could I do. While going about my duties one day, I happened to come across a new cleaner. I had never seen him before and could tell he was new by his uniform. Striking up a conversation with the cleaner I soon found out what was going on and why the clerks weren't talking.

After asking me if I was on the look out for the guys that were robbing the booth, the cleaner went on to say how the Transit Authority sent out a message to all the clerks, instructing them not to let anyone into the token booth they did not know and this especially meant police officers.

He went on to tell me the two robbers were thought to be cops or someone dressed as a cop but that most thought they were cops. He also told me that either a black or a white cop committed the robberies. They even had a shield number but the number was not a correct one. The police department had not issued the number on the shield worn by the robbers.

My eyes almost bulged out of my head when I heard this. Where did he get his information? Why didn't the cops know about this? Maybe he's pulling my leg. Either way I was going to find out.

After the cleaner finished telling me his details, I placed a call to the command. Talking to the detectives I found out what I had been told was true. They wanted to know where I learned it from but I refused to tell them. I was warned not to repeat what I had learned to anyone.

Ain't that a kick in the head the damn clerks knew more about who I should be looking for than I did. Maybe the department was doing the right thing by not informing the patrol personnel but I couldn't see how. The department was placing me and every other officer in danger. What if one of us were to walk up on these guys thinking that the robber wearing the uniform is a real police officer. We would have no idea of what hit us if they decided to take us out. Again they had the upper hand and this time it was given to them by the department.

Well, I didn't like the idea that this important piece of information was withheld, so I made sure I told every officer that I knew. So what if the information got back to the robbers, they knew it anyway. If these guys were real cops then maybe now the robberies would stop. The department could still carry on with their investigation even if the robberies did stop. Getting the word out to my fellow officers made me feel better and I knew it made them feel better. Some got angry, others filed complaints but nothing ever came from either.

Knowing more about who we were looking for and wanting to put an end to the search for a bad cop made the patrol officers work even harder. Eyeballing any officer that was not known to him or her, the officers were now spending more time checking each other out than the public. This made for some tense situations but hey, if I didn't know you, then you were worth checking out.

Thank God this did not last very long. Not more than two weeks after finding out about the uniform wearing crooks, they committed their final booth robbery. The two hit a booth that was having it's safe emptied by the revenue protection agents of the Transit Authority.

This booth was on a main station that had three smaller booth's on it and they all collected a great deal of money. Each day the smaller booths moneybags would be deposited into the safe of the main booth. While the revenue agents were removing the moneybags an officer walked up on them. Thinking nothing about the officer being there, the revenue agents went on about removing the bags.

When all the moneybags had been removed, the uniformed robber drew his gun and with the assistance of his partner that was waiting nearby, the two disarmed the group of revenue protection agents. After placing the group of revenue agents inside the booth with the clerk the robbers then fled with, heaven only knows, how much money.

That was the last time the pair was known to have robbed token booths as a team. Maybe the two split up or maybe they got caught for something else but they were never credited with another booth robbery as a team. I don't know if they were ever caught at all.

What I do know is that after the robbery spree ended, the way in which clerks and officers got along changed. No longer did the clerks look upon the officers as being a safety valve. No, for the clerks the vision of an officer in uniform was something to be leery of and it took years for that vision to change.

▼

CHAPTER 37

WHERE'S THE TRAIN?

Money isn't the only thing that people have their eyes on in the subway. Some people don't even give the money a second thought. For them, the prize to be had from the subways, are the trains themselves. Most people do not give the operator of the train any thought. All that is needed is for the train to be on time, get a seat and to reach their destination safely.

The only sight of the operator is when the train barrels into the station. For a quick second the passengers might get a glance of the operator but that's it. Seeing the conductor hanging out the window of his cab is a daily sight. The conductor is the only employee that is seen. Everyone knows in their mind that there is someone else driving the train but as long as the train reaches their station without incident, no one really cares who's driving the train.

City buses are different from trains. Each day the passengers wait for the bus, standing in the same spot at the same pickup location. Boarding the bus, most offer a good morning or hello to the driver before searching for their seat.

Getting the same bus and the same driver each day, one comes to know who is taking them on their journey. Trying to get the same seat each day, sitting next to the same person while watching as the regular passengers get on and off.

A ride on the buses of the city is quite different from a ride on the subway. Buses are smaller and hold fewer people that for some reason seem to be friendlier then the subway crowd.

On the subway, most tend to keep to themselves they don't make eye contact or talk to anyone. They find a safe spot on the platform and wait for the train. Once it does come they get on and read a book, stare, or close their eyes. They just don't talk to anyone.

Getting in the same car of the train is important. Everyone believes they have to be the closest to the stairway that leads to the street when the train reaches their station. Obtaining a seat would be nice but that's not as important as getting into a particular car. There could be seats in other cars of the train but they are not the seats wanted.

The car is the main place to be because when the train pulls into their station the passengers have to get out fast. They cannot spend one moment more than is needed in the subway. That might be pressing your luck. You made it on safely now all you gotta do is get out safely. That's the goal. Nothing else.

Subways for some reason can affect people in very different ways. The general public looks upon the subway as just a means of getting from one point to another. For others the subway is like a calling. They love being in the subway.

By paying one fare, the subway lover can ride through the entire city, each day getting more mesmerized by the system. Longing for a chance to one day operate a train, to be in charge of such a powerful piece of equipment is what they wish for, what they must have.

It's easy to spot the ones that are mesmerized by the subway. They would approach me and start talking about the system like it was a long lost love. Stating facts that no one should know or anyone cared about.

Some could tell me how long each station was, how each was built, the routes of each train while pointing out things that I nor any other person cared about. "You know what the blue light in the tunnel means? What about the yellow light? See that marker over there; you know what that's for? How fast does a train go? Bet you don't know when this station was built." These were some of the questions they would ask.

Even if I knew the answer, I would say no just to try and end the conversation to get away from the subway freak. Sometimes it worked, sometimes it didn't. Following me around the station, the person would keep up with their trivial facts. On and on the person would go, for them it couldn't get any better. They were in the subway talking to a Transit Cop, for them a dream come true.

Making my escape, I would wonder how could someone be so hooked on the subway. Get a life. There are more important things that they could spend their time doing. Why the subway?

As my time in the subway rolled along I came to notice this one guy. Everyday during rush hour I would see him standing in the window of the lead car of an "F" train. He would just be standing there looking out the window, watching the tunnel. I could set my watch by him. When his train pulled in, I knew rush hour only had thirty minutes to go. He was on time everyday and everyday he was in the same position on the same train.

Over a few weeks, I noticed the guy started to wear different pieces of the uniform that the transit employees wore. He was becoming a real buff. First there were the pants, then the shirt all the same as the transit employees except there were no emblems on them. Each time I would see him he seemed to be falling deeper and deeper into his fantasy.

One night while on patrol I was called to the crew room of a station. The locker room of the employees had been broken into and different uniforms along with keys and the handles needed to run the trains were stolen. This didn't make sense to me, why would someone steal Transit uniforms, who would want them and why?

I did not know it but my questions would be answered soon afterwards. In the train yard where the Transit Authority stored the trains that weren't being used something strange was happening. A train would be parked in a certain spot and then it would be moved without the knowledge of the train yard personnel.

At first the trains would just be moved around the yard from one position to another. The yard personnel thought one of the employees was just messing around with them to see if they would notice that the trains had been moved. They didn't give it much thought. Whoever was playing games would soon tire of it and stop, nothing to worry about.

Then came a Saturday in March, the Transit Authority reported that a train was missing from one of the storage yards. That's right, an entire train was gone and the Transit Authority had no idea as to where.

Listening to the radio was comical, "All units be on the look out for a stolen "F" train, stolen from the Transit Authority yards in Queens." They gave a description of the missing train listing all the different car numbers along with any other outstanding features. Thinking this had to be a joke, I laughed at each transmission. How could anyone steal an entire train and for what? This had to be a joke.

After about an hour of listening to the stolen train report, Central reported that the train had been found, it was in Brooklyn, and the search was called off. Once the train was located it was thought that the Transit Authority had misplaced the train. That the train was stored at the Brooklyn yard all this time and had been mistakenly reported stolen.

One week later it happened again, another train was missing. This train had not been misplaced. It was logged into the Queens storage yard only one hour before it was reported missing. The train was supposed to be in Queens but it was gone, someone had made off with it. Once again the search was on and this time it wasn't a joke.

As I stood on the platform I watched each train, hoping to spot the missing one, no luck. No one had seen the train. It was like something that large had just vanished. For hours the search went on for the train, until finally it was found again at the Brooklyn storage yard. This time the detectives were all over it. Trying to collect any type of evidence they could about who had stolen the train. Their investigation was in vain. It turned up nothing. With no clues as to who had stolen the train all the detectives could do was scratch their heads and wonder.

Thinking that they were looking for an ex-employee or a disgruntled one, the detectives started checking into each and every person who worked for or had previously worked for the Transit Authority. That investigation was going to take a long time and was leading nowhere.

The Police Department was now assigning cops to the train yards to check on every person operating a train. The hunt was on for the train thief. Weeks went by and no trains were stolen. The thought was that whomever was taking them had been scared off. Everything was back to normal. The detectives closed this investigation as an act by a disgruntled employee and moved onto other cases. They had no leads, which gave them no other choice but to move on.

Everything was fine for a month, no trains missing and no unusual problems on the system. Then it happened again but this time the stolen train wasn't missing from the storage yard, no, this train was in service. The operator of the missing train had gotten off to retrieve a package from one of the transit towers located at the end of one of his regular stops. While in the tower, someone slipped onto the train and drove off with it. The conductor did not notice and the passengers had no idea that the person operating the train was not a Transit Authority employee.

Trying their best to reach the train by radio, the Transit Authority was in a frantic turmoil. Their calls went unanswered as the train kept on rolling along. Unable to reach the person operating the train, they tried to reach the conductor. Answering the call, the conductor reported that everything was normal. The train was making all of its stops and there were no problems that he was aware of.

After advising the conductor of what happened, the Transit Authority told him that at the next station he was not to close the doors, he was to hold the train at the station and wait for the police. Agreeing to do so, he waited for the next stop to arrive, he was not going to let the train leave the station.

As the train roared into the station the conductor got ready. Only one thing was wrong, the train did not stop, it just rolled through the station. He informed the Transit Authority of what occurred and reported that at the next station he would try to hold the train. We were then rerouted to that station.

As I stood on the platform waiting for the train to arrive I wondered who would steal a train. I didn't have to wonder long, as the train entered the station I noticed that the person operating it was the buff I had seen during my patrols. "Oh shit," I thought, "I know that guy, he's nuts. He must be the one that's been breaking into the crew rooms and stealing the trains. He's a damn nut."

I watched as the train rolled past us, he had no intention of stopping. He knew we were on to him and he wasn't giving up. As the train rolled through the station, I could see the passengers now standing and looking out the windows. "Why didn't the train stop?" they must by thinking, "What's going on?"

Blowing past more and more stations without stopping, the train was making fast time. It wasn't going fast enough to trip the breaks and it kept a far enough distance from the train in front of it so as not to trip the emergency breaks. The train wasn't stopping by itself so the Transit Authority had to stop it.

The Transit Authority radioed the operator of the train in front of the stolen one and he was told to hold his train at the next station blocking the other one from being able to enter. With the station blocked we made our way over to put an end to this nut jobs ride. As the stolen train approached the station, the Transit Authority tripped its breaks. Watching as the train came to a stop I could see the buff inside of the operator's position trying his best to keep it moving. Once the train stopped we made our way aboard.

The train thief gave up without a fight and no one was injured. As he was led off the train in cuffs I asked him why he had done it? Why he endangered the lives of so many people. Without blinking an eye or hesitating he replied, "Because I could and when I get out I'm going to do it again, only then you'll never catch me." With that said he was taken away. With everything under control, the train was brought into the station and the passengers were allowed to leave.

Only a handful of them bothered to ask what happened. The most asked questions were, "How am I going to get back to my station?" "The damn train didn't make my stop, I'm not going to pay another fare to get back." "Where the hell am I?" Not realizing the danger they had been in, the angry passengers cursed and moaned as they went about finding their way back to where they wanted to be.

True to his word, the buff was right back at it when he was released from jail a few months later but this time we knew who we were looking for. The thing that sticks in my mind about this caper is not the train buff. No it's the passengers. The vision of them leaving the train without even a clue as to the danger they were in was amazing. They had no clue at all.

CHAPTER 38

▼

OLE BLUE EYES

Policing the city lead to many encounters and visions that the normal person will never see. Some were funny some were tragic but there was another one also, this was the one that the officers called the "oh-shit" syndrome. When an officer stepped into the syndrome it would have either one or two outcomes, a good one where the officer made an arrest and went home safely or badly where the officer did or didn't make an arrest but went home injured.

The syndrome comes in many shapes and sizes. There are no set ways for how the syndrome will look or act. All that is known about the syndrome is that when it does come, you gotta be ready. What is the syndrome? Well its something or someone that is looking to put fear into the officer along with the possibility of inflicting some sort of injury.

After years of working in uniform, I got another chance to put it aside and go out in plainclothes. The officers usually look upon working in plainclothes as a special assignment. Being picked for such work gives one the feeling that their work has not gone unnoticed. Most would jump at an opportunity to be a plainclothes officer.

For me, I could take it or leave it. While in uniform I felt there was no mistaking who I was and what I was doing. Everyone could see I was a cop and that I was there to keep the peace. When approaching a suspect for either a summons or to make an arrest everyone knew who I was. There was no way my identity could be challenged. The uniform took care of that.

If someone was up to no good and I was heading in their direction, with the uniform on, they would usually spot me before I saw them. Because of this, the activity the person was engaged in would stop and they would act as if nothing was going on.

I may not have seen the person doing anything but I would get the feeling that they were up to something. Even still, if I didn't see it and no one complained than there wasn't anything I could do, as long as the activity had been stopped I had done my job.

Being in uniform was fine with me. It kept me from walking into all kinds of stuff. I referred to my uniform as my silent partner, it was on my back and it had my back. My uniform was a great partner to have.

Everything changed when I accepted the plainclothes assignment. Now I didn't have my uniform, I had no silent partner. My new partner was flesh and blood, only human like me. No longer would I be able to stop wrong doings just by my presence. No longer would I be instantly recognized as an officer of the law when the time to take action arose. Being able to mix in with the public and not be recognized as a cop opened up a whole new world to me.

The last car of any train was known as the party car. If people wanted to smoke, drink, act a fool or just go nuts they went to the last car. For some reason that car was singled out for such behavior and everyone knew it. If you were looking for an exciting trip on the subway you went to the last car, it was always jumping.

Wearing my plainclothes I got to see first hand what really took place in the last car. People that didn't know each other would band together to act in any way they saw fit. Some acted as the lookout, peering into the next car, watching to see if a uniformed officer was approaching.

With the coast clear the rest of the people would start taking care of business. Playing loud radios, lighting up marijuana or cigarettes, snorting cocaine, drinking and just going wild. The party would be on until the next station was reached.

When the train pulled into a station the party would stop. No party, nothing out of the ordinary, everyone sitting still and enjoying their ride. Only the odor of the cigarettes and marijuana hung in the air. Once the doors closed the party was on again, this went on from station to station until the end of the line. It was amazing to see how people could lose their minds for a few minutes than like nothing return to normal.

Working in uniform for so many years, I never witnessed the full partying experience of the last car. Because before I could make my way into it, the party would be over. Not now, now I could watch and see for myself just what was taking place. Riding the last car of the trains my partner and I made a lot of arrests, from minor violations to felonies, it was so easy. We made so many arrests that the other officers started calling us "Starsky and Hutch."

Being labeled as the number one plainclothes team in the command, we got the best assignments. We did stakeouts, sweeps and had the freedom to roam the command area at will. To keep each other safe we had a system on how and when to approach a person. There was always eye contact with each other. We also used little hand or body movements to keep each other informed about what actions we were going to take, when to act and when not to.

Whenever the time came that we had to take police action, the rule was first the shields would come out then the words, "Police! Don't move!" If we had to, the guns would be held in hand. We had each other's back. If I were going to be frisking someone, my partner would stand back and keep an eye on the person being frisked and on me. When he did the frisking I watched him. We had no problems and clicked well. We were the perfect team.

With everything going our way we were the new untouchables, efficient and clean. Then came that night in late May. We were assigned to a stakeout looking for the guy who had been breaking into turnstiles using a crowbar. This guy had been ripping the command a new asshole. He was hitting three or four stations a night. Using a crowbar, he would break open the side of a turnstile and remove the bag containing the tokens.

Before breaking into a turnstile, he would first stuff something in the token slots of the other turnstiles, making them inoperable. With only one turnstile working, the passengers entering the station would have no choice but to use it. Being the only working turnstile the bag would fill up fast.

When he felt the bag was heavy enough, the guy would then make his move. Jamming the crowbar into the side of the turnstile he would prey open the side, remove the bag and flee to the street. By the time the clerk hit the alarm in the booth the guy would be gone.

Moving from station to station he was cleaning up. Selling the tokens for half their price he had to be making a lot of money. Once he had the tokens, getting rid of them was easy. It was well known that people were selling stolen tokens for half price and the public was not shy in buying them. This may be against the law, but a penny saved…well you know.

After reviewing the stations the guy had been striking we decided on where and when we should set up to try and catch him. He had a pattern and we thought we had figured it out. All we had to do was be at the right station at the right time.

Selecting which station to stakeout we took up our positions. The stakeout started three days before we figured the station would be hit. We did this because we wanted to make sure we knew the workings of the station well. The first night we checked our sheet to see which station we felt would be hit. As the night went along we sat and waited, nothing happening, all quiet. Were we wrong, had we made a mistake?

The answer came over the radio, a report that the guy had broken into the turnstiles of the station that we had picked. We were right, we had picked the correct station that was hit or did we just have a lucky guess. Over the next two nights we would be either proven right or wrong.

On the second night we again staked out our chosen station. Sitting and wait-ing we listened to the radio to hear if the station we suspected would be the one to get hit. If the guy struck at the station we had chosen, then we knew for sure that we were reading him right. Hour after hour we sat and waited. Then bang he hit again we were right, we had him. We knew where he was going to hit next for sure.

On the third night we were ready, taking up our positions at the Hunters Point station we went over our checklist of how we were going to take this guy down. There wasn't going to be any slip-ups. Our plan was simple we were going to let the guy do his thing. We were going to let him stuff the turnstiles and let him break into them. When he had the tokens we would spring out on him and make the arrest.

Well hidden on the station we watched the turnstiles. It was only a matter of time before he came. All we had to do was wait, so we did. As the hours went past we took turns peeking out to watch the turnstile area. Chatting, smoking and drinking coffee we waited. Every once in a while we would go over our plan again, safety first.

Relieving my partner at the watch I noticed a well-dressed man holding a bun-dle of roses standing on the mezzanine. He had on a sport jacket, shirt, tie and pressed pants. Thinking to myself that he must be waiting for a woman I disre-garded him as a suspect. Holding the flowers in his hand, he paced back and forth stopping only to observe the passengers of each train that emptied out.

"He's been waiting a long time, he must be looking for his woman," I thought. The trains came, the trains went and he waited. After about an hour I was thinking, "For him to wait this long she's gotta be nice, ain't no way he would be waiting this long if she wasn't." This woman I had to see, so I stayed at the watch, telling my partner, "I got this, just relax," I continued to watch.

Keeping my eyes on the man I saw him go over to the turnstiles. He reached into his pocket and then began to stuff the slots of the turnstiles. I told my partner what was happening and to get ready. This was the guy and he was setting up shop. After stuffing the turnstiles the man left, but we stayed. "Give it time," we told each other.

He just stuffed the turnstiles so he needed time for the tokens to build up. The time went buy and we waited. The morning rush was about to begin. With the rush would come a great deal of tokens, all placed into the one working turnstile. Once the rush got into full swing we were ready. The turnstile was filling up. It was only a matter of time.

Watching as the people made there way into the station, I noticed the man had returned. There he was standing on the side of the booth, still wearing the same outfit and holding the roses. I told my partner this is it, he's back, he's gonna hit.

As the crowd disappeared he made his way over to the turnstiles. I watched as he looked from left to right checking out the area. Then he placed the roses down on the turnstile. As he did I heard a thud. Why would the roses make such a sound? Well within the next ten seconds I got my answer.

From inside the roses the guy pulled out a crowbar, he then began working on the side of the turnstile. Yelling to my partner, "He's in, he's doing it, put it over the radio. You ready?" We were set to go into action. With the turnstile busted open he removed the heavy bag of tokens and started to make his way to the street.

Popping out from our position we made our move, not running, just walking at a normal pace we followed the guy. With a look over his shoulder he spotted us walking behind him. He must have felt something because all of a sudden be began to run.

Up the stairs he flew, us in pursuit. Reaching out I could almost touch his leg as he ran up the stairs. He was just out of reach. Up the stairs he ran, us close behind. Thinking to myself, when we hit the street unless this guy was the new 'Jessie Owens' his butt was mine. He was not going to out run me. We had him.

As we reached the top step I got prepared for the sprint. I was going to catch this guy come hell or high water. At the street level I got the shock of a lifetime. There parked right at the top of the stairs was a white Toyota pickup truck. The door flew open and in jumped the guy.

Taken back for a moment, I quickly gathered myself, out came my gun, "Police! Don't move!" I shouted while pulling on the door of the truck. Unable to open the door I started making my way around to the driver's side. Now I don't know why, maybe it was the heat of the moment but instead of going around the truck from the rear I went in front of it. I know stupid move but I wasn't thinking right at the time.

Well anyway I did it, with my gun pointed at the driver I yelled for them to get out of the truck. Focusing my eyes I realized that the driver was a woman. As I stared into her blue-green eyes, still pointing my gun and yelling for her to get out, I saw her duck down under the dashboard. The next thing I knew I heard the engine roar and could see the truck start towards me. The "oh-shit" syndrome hit me.

She was going to run me over. With that in mind, I threw out my hand and pushed myself away from the truck. With the force of the truck, I was thrown about fifteen feet, landing on my rear. With me sailing through the air the truck took off, all I saw was the flashing red taillights.

Clearing my head I then spotted my partner standing in the street, gun drawn, he asked, "Are you alright, you ok?" Stating that I was, I got to my feet, still not believing what had just happened. We put out a description of the truck and its occupants but the two had gotten away.

We didn't make the arrest but we weren't injured so everything was alright. We'll get them next time. We did not know then there would not be a next time. After that night the break-ins stopped, the pair did not strike again. Why, we didn't know but they had stopped.

The answer came about a month later when we got a call from some detectives in Manhattan. They arrested a woman on a petty charge and she wanted to give up some information in exchange for the charge being dropped.

What she said was her roommate and another person had been robbing turnstiles around the city and that one night the two tried to run down a cop. That cop was me. A deal was cut and the two were arrested.

As the woman and man were led into the courtroom I looked again into her blue-green eyes. With a smile on her face she stared back at me before saying, "Hey, it's you, you're that cop." Rising up on her toes she went on to say, "Oh, what a feeling, Toyota," she then began to laugh while still bouncing on her toes. Well, I got the final laugh. The pair was found guilty and sentenced to jail.

The vision of her eyes staring at me as I heard the roar of the trucks engine will never go away. That night I got lucky and I know it. We were good but I'll take luck over being good any day.

▼

CHAPTER 39

COMMUNICATIONS DOWN

When the syndrome hits it stays around for a while. There's no such thing as a one time hit. When it rains it pours. The syndrome comes in spurts that can last anywhere from a week to months. Our turn had come. Being good at what we did had no affect on the syndrome. We were in the grip of this uncaring monster and it wasn't letting go.

Trying to ignore the run of events that had been coming our way, we went about working to the best of our abilities. Still the number one plainclothes team in the command, we were getting the best assignments. We were called into the Captain's office one day to go over another crime spree that had started in our area.

Telephones on the stations were being broken into and their coin boxes were being stolen. Almost every telephone on the system within the command had been vandalized. With the rash of telephone break-ins it was hard for the public to find a working telephone on the subway. Having working telephones is a must.

The stations can be a frightening place to be. Late at night on a lonely platform people tend to stand next to the phones just in case something happened and they needed to call for help. Telephones made the public feel safe.

With the working telephones only an arms length away a call could be made in seconds. Women, men, kids, they all stood next to the telephones because no one is immune to what can befall them on the subway.

Having been given the assignment of putting an end to the telephone bandit my partner and I started gathering as much information as possible. We read the reports filed by other officers. We interviewed the clerks and cleaners of the stations. We inspected the phones that had been broken into, trying to get a feel for how the person was operating.

Most of the information that we gathered was of no use. Some phones had been broken into on the mezzanine next to the token booths. Each clerk we spoke with said they did not see a thing. The cleaners gave the same stories. They had seen nothing as they moved around the stations scrapping the dirt left behind by the public.

The telephones gave us our best lead though. From examining the broken frames, we came to the conclusion that the object being used was either a small pry bar or a large screwdriver. It had to be something along those lines because from what we saw of the phones, the sides had been peeled away and there were a lot of jagged edges.

A hammer was not used because it would create noise and draw attention to the theft. From the looks of the phones, to break into them would take quite some time. They were made of harden steel and getting into them was not easy. Whoever the thief was, he or she would have to spend a few minutes working on the sides to gain entry to the coin box.

With every public phone made inoperable by the bandit the phone company had to repair or replace them. The cost of replacing a phone is very high and the cost of repairing a phone isn't that much cheaper. Replacing the entire phone cost twenty-five hundred dollars. Repairing the phone could range from fifty dollars to the twenty-five hundred mark and with the number of phones that were vandalized, the price tag was steep.

Offering a reward for information leading to the arrest and conviction of anyone vandalizing their equipment the phone company hoped to get help from the public in catching the person or persons responsible for the damage. We didn't need to be offered a reward. It was our job to catch the person and we set out to do so.

Meeting with the representatives from the phone company, a plan was being developed as to how we were going to lure and trap the telephone bandit. Settling on an idea we put the plan in motion. Having the phone company refit the subway phones with another type of coin box cover, one that is thicker, harder and almost impossible to remove, the plan was moving forward. Outfitting the phones with the new covers took time so the going was slow, that gave us more time to refine our plan.

With the new phone covers ready to be installed, we advised the phone company to place the new covered phones on certain stations only. The old style phones would be left on the other stations. Each day the phone company would replace phones on the chosen stations until all but four stations were left with the old type.

With the phones in place all we had to do was give random checks to the stations and note if any attempt had been made to break into the phones. Twenty-four hours a day uniformed officers covered the four stations that contained the older-type phones. Therefore, we felt the thief would make his attempt on one of the new phones.

Each day my partner and I ran checks on the phones. The plan was working. While inspecting the newer phones, we found scratches and other marks on them. Someone tried to pry the boxes out but was unable to. Going from station to station, we found the same type of marks on each and every phone.

Now was the time to spring the trap. Having the officers moved from the four stations with the old phones we then set up shop on them. Knowing that it would only be a matter of time before the guy hit, we had to come up with a way to pick the correct station. At this time we had a one-in-four chance of being right. Bouncing between the stations we would spend two hours at each, hoping that nothing happened on the other three.

We went back and forth between the stations for two weeks with no results. The guy wasn't hitting. Maybe he moved to another area, maybe we lost him? Another week went by and still nothing, no sign of the bandit. With no break-ins taking place, the department felt there wasn't a need for my partner and myself to be working the case, so they pulled us off it. With the four stations now uncovered it only took a matter of days before the guy struck.

On the third day after being reassigned we just happened to stop by one of the four stations to inspect the phones. On the station we found every phone had been vandalized. Six phones had their coin boxes removed. We found the same thing at each of the other three stations. Every phone that had not been refitted with the new cover had been broken into.

He was back and making up for lost time. Again we moved to set our plan. With the phone company cooperating with us we were sure the end was near for the telephone bandit.

Arrangements were made to have the phones located on the four stations repaired on the same day. The phones would be repaired but only one station would have operating phones and on that station my partner and I would wait. With uniformed officers doing train patrol throughout the area, if the guy did strike we had more than enough back up to assist. Taking up our positions at 170th street on the "D" line we settled in for a long night.

We could observe almost the entire station from our hiding spots. It wasn't very large and was the ideal location for our purpose. No one knew we were there, not the clerk, the cleaner, the public and not even the train patrol officers. They were only told there were plainclothes officers in the given area. The uniformed officers were told to use caution when coming upon a situation.

My partner and I kept in contact using the radios to talk with each other. The station was quiet and the night came to a crawl. With the talk around button on the radio, any conversation that we had could not be heard by Central. We tried to keep each other alert by cracking jokes on each other and talking about nothing of importance.

This went on for a good three hours before I heard my partner say, "Hey, I got a guy over here, this is the third time I've seen him." "What's he doing?" I asked. Pausing my partner then said, "He's walking up and down the platform, looks like he's checking out the phones." Leaving my position, I told my partner to keep an eye on the guy, I was on my way.

Before I could reach my partner a train entered the station and the male left. Giving me a description of the male, my partner also filled me in on what he thought the male might be up to. Before we finished our conversation, another train from the opposite direction entered the station. Waiting for the passengers to exit before going back to my position, I noticed a guy fitting the description that I was just given coming down to the platform.

"Look, is that the guy?" I asked. "Yes, that's him," my partner said. With our eyes fixed on him we watched the guy move about the platform. His movements were suspicious, head moving from side to side, stopping and checking every sound. We felt he was up to no good. With the station clear of passengers the guy again started looking around.

This time he came right over to the spot where we were hidden. Pulling on the doorknob while trying to see inside through vents in the door. He was making sure the coast was clear. Not having a reason to be suspicious of the door, he moved over to the telephone located no more than ten feet away.

From his right rear pocket I observed the male remove a large screwdriver and a small pry bar. Taking a final look over his shoulder, he turned back to the phone. I could see his hands moving and he seemed to be applying pressure from his lower body, pushing off with his legs. This was it. He was breaking into the phone. "Get ready," I said to my partner, "Let's see how many he's gonna hit."

There were five phones on the platform and as we watched he ripped open each one. Having completed his crime, the guy started to make his way up the stairs. This gave my partner and I the time needed to exit from our location without being seen.

Thinking he must be headed for the street, we went upstairs in search of him. To our surprise he was standing at the top of the stairway, he was waiting for the train. My partner gave me a signal that I should go back down while he made the approach on the guy from up top.

Not to raise the suspicion of the male as to why I was all of a sudden going back downstairs, I started patting my pockets as if I had lost something. Stating, "Hold on, I dropped my keys," to my partner. I turned and headed back down. "Wait here I'll be right back," I said.

Walking past the guy at the top of the stairs, I headed down. Just as I reached the bottom my partner made his move. In a loud voice I heard him say, "Police don't move!" Spinning around I could see the guy now headed in my direction. Out came my shield followed by me also shouting, "Police don't move!" Trapped between the two of us he had no place to go.

Taking control of the guy, I placed him against the wall and started to conduct a frisk. With my partner watching my back I knew I was alright. So I focused on the guy. Going about frisking I was locked into every movement that the guy might make.

My partner was easy to identify as a cop, with his gun in hand and shield hanging from his neck, radio sticking out of his rear pocket along with the color of the day on his wrist. That's the secret color that is chosen each day by the department for the plainclothes cops to wear so that the uniformed officers can identity them. My partner had my back and with the proper display of his equipment anyone approaching would be able to tell that he was a cop, or so we thought.

From behind us we heard, "Police don't move!" Now I'm thinking, "That's not my partners voice, who's that?" Before I could turn, the voice again stated, "Police don't move, drop the gun!!" Now I knew it wasn't my partner I was hearing. "You, asshole, I said drop the gun!!" the voice said again.

Now the "oh-shit" syndrome hit me. One of the train patrol officers had us at gunpoint. He was thinking that my partner and I were criminals robbing this guy! We were so focused on making the arrest we had not heard a train enter the station. Not wanting to make a move, I heard my partner say, "Hey guy, we're on the job! Look there's my shield, there's my radio, can't you see the color?

No, the uniformed officer was locked in. He had tunnel vision. The only thing he could see was the gun. "I'm not telling you again," he said, "Drop the goddamn gun." While holding onto the male with a firm grip I told my partner, "Just do as he says, drop the gun before he shoots us."

I should have expected the answer that I got back because it was something that most cops would say. "I'm not dropping shit," my partner said, "I'll put the gun down, but I ain't dropping shit. You know how much this thing cost?"

Agreeing to let my partner lay his gun down instead of dropping it, the uniformed officer watched as the gun was placed on the ground. He then ordered my partner to get on the wall, legs spread while still telling us not to move or he would shoot us. He called for backup over his radio. I heard him say he had three men at gunpoint. One of them armed with a gun, possible robbery suspects.

My mind is thinking fast now. I told the guy we were trying to arrest "You better not move. This cop might shoot all of us." With his eyes as big as flying saucers he just shook his head. "Officer, look at my shield, can't you see my shield," my partner kept saying. I gave the name of our command, what unit we were working and our supervisor's name. Nothing was getting through to the officer.

Taking a look over my shoulder I could see the officer standing behind a column, gun in hand and it was pointed at my back. As if all this wasn't bad enough, I also noticed the officer was a rookie and the gun was shaking in his hands. One slip and bang someone could be shot. All I thought was, "Be cool, keep talking and just be cool." Keep trying to get it through to the officer that we are cops.

The few minutes that it took for the backup officers to arrive seemed like years. When the troops did arrive, the relief I felt was wonderful when I heard someone say to the rookie, "You idiot, those guys are cops. What the hell are you doing, put that gun away!" Once the situation was under control I could have collapsed from the release of the pressure.

After gathering ourselves, we went looking for the uniformed officer that just seconds ago had us in the sights of his gun. Finding the cop I had just a few questions for him. "How the hell didn't he see our shields, and the color of the day? Had he not heard our radios also blaring away? What the hell was he thinking?"

His answer was simply, "My bad," as he walked away. "My bad," that's it, that's all he had to say. I wanted to break my foot off in his ass that would have been "My bad."

It took a long time for me to bring myself to talk to the officer again, but we smoothed things over and put the incident behind us. Even with the incident long past I still have the vision of the rookie officer frozen in position, blank look on his face and gun in hand ready to blow us away. He was frozen by tunnel vision.

CHAPTER 40

▼

BLINDERS

Saying that this was the last time we would be in the grip of the syndrome would not be true. There was more to come and with each the tension was to get stronger. Not wanting to slip up the two of us would go over different situations that we might run into.

Everyday, whenever we had a moment we would cover such things as being held at gunpoint again, chasing a criminal, not separating from each other and always being in eye contact. Take downs would go by the book. One of us would cover and give instructions while the other would make the frisk and cuff.

After being in the grip of the syndrome so many times and getting out without a scratch, we felt it may be only a matter of time before we might not be able to escape the syndrome safely. Reviewing how we did our job gave us more confidence in our tactics and ourselves.

Using the knowledge of what we learned was working. The arrests were made without a hitch and when it came to teamwork, we were as if of one mind. Taking the time after each roll call to speak to the uniform officers also helped.

Before turning out to patrol, my partner and I would stand in front of the officers and say, "You guys know us and we know you, but sometimes in the heat of conflict we don't think right, so take a good look at us, this is what we are wearing tonight."

After giving the officers a chance to look us over we than told them the area where we would be working. Taking this precaution would make the night go smoothly. There should be no mistaking us for criminals.

Everything was going as planned, over the next few months we did not even come close to the syndrome. With our confidence high, there seemed to be no condition we could not handle.

Officers come and officers go. Changing command is often done. With the movement come new and fresh faces. Whenever a new face came into the command my partner and I made sure the officer knew who we were. Either in the command or out on the road, whenever we came across a new face we introduced ourselves.

This was done with the supervisors also. They had to know us also. An assigned officer drives around most supervisors in a patrol car because most officers know their patrol areas better than the supervisors.

The reason for the supervisors not knowing the area covered is easy to answer. When an officer is promoted to supervisor he or she is then transferred to another command to horn their skills. Being new to the position, the department felt the new supervisors would learn faster if they worked with officers not known to them. Playing favorites was out. Not having a relationship with their new officers would make it easier if the supervisor had to take disciplinary actions against one of them.

Very few new supervisors stayed in their old commands, we were lucky enough to have one of them. The new Sergeant was someone I worked with for over six years. He wasn't one of my favorites but he knew us and we knew him. There should be no breaking-in period, he didn't have to learn us and we didn't have to learn him.

Greeting the new Sergeant at his first roll call I started to notice something was different about him. He was starting to take the job very seriously. He had changed. Whatever the department put in his head while training him to be a Sergeant started to turn him against the officers. Acting more like a drill Sergeant, he would bark out orders to the troops.

One of his favorite sayings when addressing the troops was, "When I used to be a cop…" Whenever he spoke to us he would use that phrase. Saying things like, "When I used to be a cop, I did this and I did that, so I know how the game is played. I've been there and nothing gets by me."

What did he mean by, "When I used to be a cop?" What is he now? I know he's a Sergeant, but he's still a cop. He's a supervisor of cops but he's still a cop. After listening to him say this one time too many for me I asked him, "Sarge, just what do you mean by that? I know you got stripes and wear a gold shield. I know you're a Sergeant but what do you mean by saying when you used to be a cop?"

Knowing that he was about to cut into me, I wanted to get my monies worth. Adding, "What, you can't arrest people anymore? You can't write a ticket? If someone needed help and saw you, you wouldn't be able to help them because you're not a cop? Just explain to me exactly what you are?

Seeing the fire build up in him, he answered back, "I'm a supervisor, I tell you what to do. I don't have to write tickets or make arrests that's your job, understand?" Not satisfied I kept on asking, "Are you a cop or not, yes or no, give me a simple answer!" His answer would say it all. "No, I'm not a cop. I'm a supervisor, a Sergeant, now do you understand!

Yes, I did understand, his head had gotten big. He got lucky on a Saturday and passed the Sergeant's test now he was mister big stuff. Better than a cop but lower than a lieutenant. Now I knew where the officers stood with him.

After working with someone for so many years and getting to know them it was hard to see how something like being made Sergeant could change a person. Over the months he distanced himself further and further away from the officers. He was large and in charge.

Giving him the respect the gold shield deserved, I would only talk to him about job related matters. I had no choice because if the subject weren't job related he would ignore me completely. Not just me but any and every officer that might have something to say.

The new Sergeant was really living up to the old adage that the higher you go up within the department the more brain dead you become. He was living proof this was true. Not letting him get to us my partner and I kept on doing what we did best.

Before going out on patrol, my partner and I would check with the new Sergeant to see if he wanted to make any changes. To find out if the Sergeant had something other in mind for us to do that day. With his approval we would than make our way out the door.

One day after going about our routine at the command we headed out to patrol. Bopping around, the Parsons Blvd/Archer Ave. station we found little going on. There weren't any police conditions to handle and the day was dragging. Covering this station was not our idea. The Sergeant had placed us here.

For some reason he wanted us to cover this station for the entire tour, eight hours on one station. Even in plainclothes, being assigned to one station for an entire tour sucked. Sooner or later the public would catch on to us and our cover would be blown.

No one except cops, employees or bums would hang around a station for so long. Looking at us, people could tell we weren't employees or bums, so that left cops. This made for a very long day. Our only way out was to make an arrest and from the way the day was going, that didn't seem likely.

While sitting on the platform trying to figure out why we had been assigned to this hellhole of a station, we spotted the uniformed officers that were also covering the station. The post cops were two female rookies and they were happy to see my partner and I.

Talking to the officers, we learned that one of them overheard the Sergeant telling the Lieutenant that he wanted to give my partner and I, Parsons Blvd./ Archer Ave. station because he didn't like our attitude and he wanted to slap us back a notch.

Now this one was easy to figure out. The Sergeant was upset with us because I told him my opinions. Whatever he had in store for us we could handle. Making the best of a bad situation was nothing new to us. We could handle it.

With nothing going on at the station we longed for the day to end. Then over the radio we heard a call of a man armed with a gun on a train that was in the station. I asked Central for a complete description of the person and for an exact location on the train. After receiving the response we took out our color of the day bands along with our shields and guns and began searching the train.

Radio in hand, listening for any updates we made our way through the train. Weaving in and out of the cars we had our eyes peeled for the guy. Over the radio I heard that other officers were responding to the station.

Taking nothing for granted, my partner told Central to notify the responding officers that we were on the station conducting a search for the guy and to alert them of our description, just to be safe. Central put the information we requested out over the air. Now we were certain everyone knew we were there and what we looked like.

As we entered the fifth car we spotted a guy that fit the description of the man with the gun. The guy was leaning on a seat staring at another male. He had his right hand under his jacket and was making threatening remarks to the other guy.

I made my approach from his left. My partner came from his right. Walking as if nothing was going on we made our way over to the threatening male. He paid no attention to us and just kept on staring at the other guy. Once we got within reach we moved fast. Jumping on the guy from both sides we grabbed him while yelling, "Police, don't move, keep your hands where we can see them!"

The fight was on. Trying our best to keep the males hands still, I held onto his left arm while my partner held his right. Off the train we went still struggling with the guy. Once on the platform we took him down to the ground. He was still reaching inside of his jacket and we knew he was going for the gun.

Holding the male down with my left hand while sitting on his legs, I retrieved my gun from its holster. While pointing my gun at him I told him, "Don't reach, keep your hands still!" Seeing my gun aimed at him he froze, which enabled my partner to take the male's gun out of his waistband.

After securing the guy's gun, we were about to cuff him when all of a sudden I heard the female officers voices, they were yelling, "Sarge no, Sarge their cops, Sarge!!" Turning our heads we could see the Sergeant taking aim at us, he had us locked in the sights of his gun.

Passengers on the train ducked for cover. My eyes fixed on the Sergeant's eyes they were blank, that oh-shit feeling shot through my body. I said, "Sarge, it's me, Sarge we got him, Sarge what the hell you doing?" There was no change in his actions, he continued to circle, still aiming his gun at us. Nothing was getting through to him.

As the female officers continued to yell at the Sergeant, I began to roll to my right, with my gun now aimed at the Sergeant I was ready. My partner also had his gun aimed at the Sergeant. This was bad, as bad as it could get without any-one being shot.

Applying pressure on the male to hold him down at the same time we were in a standoff with the Sergeant, my thoughts were, "If he shoots my partner I'm going to shoot him," and I was hoping my partner was thinking the same. Any-way you looked at it someone was going to get shot.

This couldn't be happening but it was. Watching the Sergeant circle us we kept on trying to reach him. "Sarge it's us, Sarge put the gun away, Sarge don't you recognize us?" With us yelling at him and the female officers screaming at him also, the message finally got through. Lowering his gun he said, "Jesus, guys I'm sorry, I didn't recognize you. Jesus guys I'm sorry."

With everything under control now we finished cuffing our prisoner. While we did this the Sergeant kept saying, "Jesus, guys forgive me, I'm sorry, I didn't mean it," over and over he kept repeating the same thing.

My comment to him was very simple, "Sarge," I said, "We have known each other for over six years and you've been our supervisor for over nine months, how the hell could you not recognize us, that's bull! I wish you had shot one of us because we were going to light your ass up. Shooting one of us was going to be the last thing you ever did. Now do you understand that!"

After this incident, the Sergeant started to change back into the nice guy that he used to be. He was becoming a cop again, not just a supervisor that was out of touch with his personnel. The more he changed, the easier it was to work with him and the more the officers came to respect him as a person, not just as a Sergeant.

Having come that close to being shot by a fellow officer again or having to shoot a fellow officer scared the hell out of me. The "oh-shit" syndrome had moved to another level and the vision of the Sergeant ready to shoot us has haunted me ever since.

CHAPTER 41

▼

THE NUMBERS GAME

Having escaped another close encounter with the grim reaper one would think that putting an end to my plainclothes assignment would have been the smart thing to do. Believe me I did consider it. I did want out and I told the Captain that enough was enough, and that I wanted to go back to uniform.

For a few days all I wanted was to put back on my uniform and get back to normal. With my uniform I was safe. Everyone would know me. I wouldn't have to worry about the criminals and the cops at the same time.

Worrying about criminals that may want to take me out of the picture was bad enough. When I added the cops to the mix that just put my chances of being hurt over the top. So for me, at that moment, I'd had enough of the plainclothes.

Not wanting to lose me, the Captain said my partner and I could work in uniform for a few days while we thought things through. We were not to be given any particular stations, we could go anywhere within the command we wanted. All we had to do was let the Sergeant know where we wanted to go and that was it.

His offer was accepted, so we took the time off from plainclothes. For the four days I was back in my uniform I did absolutely nothing. Writing a ticket was out of the question, making an arrest was the last thing on my mine. I needed to think.

Talking with my partner, we decided to give the plainclothes one more shot. Telling me, "Look, what happened was not our fault. Things are going to happen and no matter how hard we try to stop them or hide from them they are still going to take place. Not working in plainclothes wasn't going to keep fate from finding us. We're good at what we do and we should keep on doing it. I don't want to leave plainclothes and I don't want to work with someone else, so please give it just one more try, for me, please."

How could I let him down? Back to the plainclothes I went but this time I was more leery about everyone and everything than I ever was before. Was I losing my touch, were my nerves shot, had I lost my zest for the assignment? I didn't know. There was so much going through my mind that I couldn't figure things out, but I had to. For the safety of my partner and myself I had to pull myself together.

The first couple of arrests that we made after going back were treated with kid gloves. Going by the book and beyond, before approaching anyone, I would make sure every piece of equipment I carried was displayed in full view.

Never again would I stare down the barrel of a fellow officers gun. Never again would I have that oh-shit feeling placed in me by another officer. No, everyone was .going to know who we were, there would be no doubt about it.

Taking these extra precautions was working out great. Some of the other officers would say I was going overboard and call me a 'Nervous Nelly.' But what did I care, this is my life, and the life of my partner. I was doing what I felt necessary to keep us safe.

Screw the others, if they wanted to act like "Super Cops" let them, not us. At the end of our tours we were going home. Not just going home but going home with the same amount of holes in our bodies that we came to work with.

Working with our new heighten safety standards went well. We seemed to be more efficient and were getting even better then we had been. Taking down criminals was second nature to us. We got to the point where it seemed nothing could go wrong.

With the crime rate down in the command, we were called into the Captains office once again. Wondering what he wanted with us, my partner and I made our way to the office. Asking each other, "What did you do?" we hesitated outside the door before going in. Each of us answered the same, "I didn't do anything, so what could he want with us?" after shrugging our shoulders we went in.

Sitting at his desk with a mound of papers in front of him, the Captain looked up at us. "You guys know why I called you in here?" he asked. At the same time we answered, "No." A strange look came over the Captain's face. Sitting back in his chair he stated, "I've heard that you guys were like the Bopsie twins, but damn, you even speak the same words at the same time."

Shaking off his look of amazement, he went on to say that he needed us to write some tickets for him. Crimes being committed were down and so were the tickets being issued. Crime being down was a good thing but the tickets being down weren't.

Everyone in the police department has to produce, be it by making arrests or writing tickets. Everyone has to come up with numbers. Month after month the numbers game is played and you're only as good as your last months total.

Not wanting to call the numbers game a quota, the department came up with names like an, "Officer's expectation" or "Goal for the month." Missing your goal could lead to being removed from your chosen assignment, not being approved for days off or being given the worst assignments within your command.

If the expectation wasn't met for months at a time, it could lead to the officer being reassigned to another command. That was the worst thing that could happen because no one wanted to be transferred without their request for one.

Not even the Captain was safe from the numbers game. Having to go to meetings known as "Comstock" each month, he too was raked over the coals by the Chiefs. Each month's numbers were compared against the numbers of the previous year. The Captain was expected to have his command's numbers better then the previous year.

With the crime totals down and still falling, he was doing fine in that area but the tickets were another issue. He needed to raise the numbers. He had to bring the command up to or past what was written the previous year or risk feeling the wrath of the Chiefs. For him to reach his goal he needed my partner and I to write tickets. Since there weren't any major crimes for us to go after, he wanted tickets and he wanted them now.

Coming from the Captain this was not a request, this was an order and we could not refuse it. Writing tickets was fine with me, it would make the days go by faster while giving us something to do other than sitting around waiting for someone to commit a crime, which wasn't happening.

With a fresh book of tickets each we headed out to fulfill our given task. Like I said writing tickets was easy. Being in plainclothes, we were able to observe all sorts of violations. The tickets were coming fast and furious, we were writing a book each a day.

With his numbers increasing, the Captain was a happy man. You could tell by the way he walked around the command and by the way he spoke. He was on cloud nine. With crime down, tickets up and rising there was nothing negative that could be said to him at the next "Comstock" meeting.

We were making his life easy and he was doing the same for us. Not searching for crimes only, being able to write tickets was really making the days go quickly. The job was becoming fun again.

CHAPTER 42

▼

PUBLIC ENEMY

Issuing tickets to people isn't fun. But watching how they committed certain violations then listening to the stories they came up with to justify their actions was fun. For each violation committed, there was a different reason as to why it was done.

The stories went on and on. Most of the time after listening to the reason why the violation was committed, my partner and I could make a person laugh at themselves for doing what they had done or the manner in which they did it. Even though we were giving the person a ticket we didn't have to make them feel bad.

Writing tickets was safer for my partner and myself. We were just dealing with violators not criminals. So we didn't have to be on guard all the time, famous last words.

With the ticket issuing going along smoothly we were feeling pretty good. Then came that Saturday at Junction Blvd on the # 7 line. We had written about half a book of tickets each and were getting ready to call it a night. While standing on the mezzanine awaiting the train we observed a male jump over the turnstile, he was going to be our last ticket of the day.

As he headed up the stairway to the platform we called him back. Turning towards us, the male started cursing and waving his arms. "Look guy," I said, "You're only gonna get a ticket there's no reason to get upset." Still cursing, the male made his way over to us. "Give me your identification and you'll be outta here in a minute," I told him.

His response was blunt, "Fuck you, I don't have none. Get the fuck away from me, I'll just leave!" Now maybe with a better attitude we would have let him leave but not now, not after cursing us out. No, he was going to get a ticket at the least.

Again I asked for his identification and again I got cursed at. He made up my mind for me. I was going to arrest him now. Telling the male he was under arrest, I started to reach for my handcuffs when all of a sudden the male took a punch at my partner.

The fight was on! We fought tooth and nail for what seemed like an eternity. It was two against one and should have been over quickly but no, this guy was fighting like he just committed a murder.

Having taken him off his feet we now struggled with him on the floor. Cuffing him was not going to be easy. Every time we pulled his hands from under him, he fought to get them back to his front. I heard my partner say, "He's got something in his waistband, don't let him get his hands in there!"

Holding on for dear life I gripped the man's right arm, my partner was pulling on his left arm. After a few more minutes of fighting we finally got the man cuffed. Standing him up, we placed him against the wall and started to search him, looking for whatever it was he was trying so desperately to get from his waist.

My eyes lit up as my partner removed a loaded colt revolver from the man's waist. Once we had the gun we thought we knew why he was fighting so hard, he didn't want to be caught with it. He didn't want to go to jail for carrying an unlicensed gun.

After unloading the gun I told the man, "Well now you're going away for a long time. You should have just given me your identification, you would have been on your way, how stupid can you get?"

Having said this, the guy looked at us, took a spit on the floor and stated, "I should have shot you when I first saw you. I knew you were cops. I should have just shot you both!" His eyes were dark and his speech was harsh. I could tell that he meant every word he was saying.

Back at the command we ran his name through the computer, what came out sent a chill up my spine. This guy wasn't just a fare beat with a gun. He was wanted for murder, robbery and rape.

The precinct had been looking for him for over eight months. He robbed a grocery store, killed the owner and then raped the wife of the owner. This guy was bad and he needed to be taken off the streets. Now he was and I was happy about being the one to do so.

As I prepared my paperwork he stared at me from his cell. He didn't blink, just stared. When he spoke he gave me a warning. "I don't care how long it takes, I don't care how long I'm in jail but one day I'm gonna get out and when I do, I'll find you and I'll kill you. Remember what I'm telling you because before I die, I'm going to kill you like I should have done tonight." With his dark eyes still glaring at me he sat back and laughed. Saying over and over again, "I'll get you, one day I'll get you."

For his crimes the man was given forty-years-to-life in prison, so I didn't have to worry about him making good on his threats. By the time he was to get out of prison, if he ever did, I would be retired and probably living in another state so his threats meant nothing to me. I had done my job. He was going to rot in prison. That would be the end of him.

I didn't let the empty threats made by the guy get to me but I still remember them. The vision of his dark eyes staring at me from the cell, threatening to kill me, I still see to this day. Every once in a while I look over my shoulder, just in case.

That was it, no more plainclothes for me. No way, no how was I going to continue working in an assignment that kept placing me in more danger than was necessary. With my mind made up, the dream team of plainclothes went their separate ways.

CHAPTER 43

▼

WHERE'S THE JUSTICE

Getting back into uniform was just what I needed. The pressure was off me now and I was feeling fine. Even the air that I breathed smelled better than usual, if it's possible for the air in the subway to smell good. To me, the relief of not having to worry about the public and the cops was wonderful. I was back in my uniform and loving it.

Working alone didn't bother me. I did what I wanted, when I wanted. If I wanted to write a ticket I did. If I wanted to make an arrest I would just wait for someone to do something worth arresting them for.

My days flew by, even if I worked overtime before or after the regular tour the day seemed to pass quickly. When I got involved in situations where I had to place someone under arrest, they were handled without incident. The person being arrested knew who I was and why they were being arrested.

The public could see that I was a cop, not a criminal trying to rob or assault the person. If the need for assistance came up, the responding officers did not mistake me for the bad guy. Yes, everyone knew who I was and that's what I wanted. My world was back in order and I was taking advantage of it.

One day while going about my patrol at the Court Square station, I took up a position directly in front of the turnstiles. It was rush hour. I wanted as many people as possible to see me on the station.

Being highly visible kept a lot of stupid things from taking place. If the public saw me, that would lessen the chance of someone committing a crime. If there weren't any crimes committed on my station than I had done my job.

With rush hour moving along and the station quiet, I spent the majority of my time greeting the passengers and giving out directions. Not once had I removed my ticket book from my pocket. The radio was quiet and the people were friendly. How could I ask for more? Now this was how I liked it. No problems, no need to take action.

The people came and went, most of them not even giving me a second thought. With the day going the way it was I started thinking about meal. What was I going to eat? Chinese food, fried chicken or a burger they all sounded good. Just thinking about them made me even hungrier. Settling on the chicken, I could hardly wait. I could almost taste the chicken and it was driving me nuts.

Finally, rush hour was over, now the munching could begin. As I headed towards the turnstiles to leave I noticed an older man around fifty years old standing at the first wheel. He looked at me, mumbled something then manipulated the turnstile backwards while slipping through it without paying.

My eyes lit up, he must be out of his mind I thought. He saw me. He knew I saw him, so why did he do that right in front of me? Why now, I wanted my chicken and he was stopping me from getting it.

Saying to myself, "Ok he's an older guy, maybe he really didn't see me. Maybe he has cataracts or something. I'll just correct the situation by giving him a warning and then go get my chicken."

Calling out to the man, I received no response. He just kept walking away from me. Again I called him back, this time in a more forceful voice. Still nothing, he continued to walk away. I knew he heard me and chose to ignore my call. That pissed me off. He was getting a ticket now, so away I went. Walking fast, I caught up to the man. Strolling along with him I asked, "Sir, why didn't you pay your fare back there? Do you have a problem or something?"

Now over the years I have been cursed out plenty of times by plenty of people but this guy was something special. He stopped walking and took up a boxer's stance while glaring at me. The next thing I knew he let the curses fly. Starting off with your mother this and your mother that, he was ripping me a new asshole. Each and every word that came out of his mouth was foul. In amazement I stood there listening to the man as he ranted on.

Trying to interject my comments into his barrage of insults I said, "Sir, there's no need for that kind of language. Please clam down." Saying this didn't help at all, in fact it seemed to fire him up more. With his voice getting louder and the curses ringing out in the station, the few stragglers left over from the rush hour crowds couldn't help but stop and take notice of what was going on.

Feeling that I had to put an end to his ranting as quickly as possible, I stopped him in mid curse and asked for his identification. "Fuck you," is what he said, "If you want my ID then take it. Come on you pussy take it, I'll kick your ass!"

That feeling was coming over me again. Why was this guy so upset? It's only a ticket and he knew he deserved it. I had been polite and had not raised my voice to him. All I did was confront him for not paying his fare. He was making more out of this than was necessary, now it was up to me to put an end to it.

Waiting for my reaction, the older man stood in front of me ready for a fight. I didn't want to fight him. All I wanted was to write the ticket then get my chicken. Not being able to calm the man down, I knew I would have to arrest him. Telling him he left me no other choice but to do so I made my move.

Grabbing the male by his left arm, I spun him around and proceeded to try and cuff him. The cuffing was not going to be easy. This old guy was strong. With every tug I gave on his arm, he would tighten up while trying to wrestle free. Breaking away from my grasp he turned on me. Taking up his stance again, he threw a right hand at me. His punch bounced off the shock plate in my bullet-proof vest without doing any harm.

I followed his punch with a right hand of my own. Landing flush on his face I could hear the smack of flesh hitting flesh. As he recoiled backwards, still throwing punches I knew he was stunned. Seeing my opening I tore into him like a windmill in a hurricane. Raining blows upon him while blocking or dodging most of his, I had him on the ropes.

As we fought back towards the booth area I was hitting him as hard as I could. With each blow I landed he would let out a grunt, but he wasn't going down. This was a fight that I had to win. A cop cannot afford to lose, because if I lost the fight I might also have lost my life.

With the fight raging on the mezzanine I could hear my radio calling out, "10/ 13, Court Square station on the G line!" The clerk had seen the fight and called it in for me. Knowing that help was on the way, I continued fighting with the man.

Every time he hit me I would hit him back. On and on the fight went until I landed a crushing blow to his right jaw. With my blow finding its mark, he fell to one knee and I jumped on him. Having gotten one cuff on his left arm I was getting the upper hand. I was getting the upper hand but had not gotten it yet.

As I pulled on the cuffs he still fought with his free hand. Face down on the mezzanine he kept reaching back with his right hand. All of a sudden I felt a tug on my holster. He was reaching for my gun. Feeling him pulling at my gun sent me into another level of the "oh-shit" syndrome.

I held onto his cuffed wrist with all my strength while securing my gun with my right hand. Giving a quick upward snap of the holster, I trapped his hand between it and the gun. The pain caused by the holstered gun squeezing his hand made him yell out, the more he yelled the harder I squeezed.

Pulling on the cuffs while squeezing his hand at the same time I was finally getting control of him. Not being able to withstand the pain any longer he said, "Ok, ok I give up, get the fuck off me!" I released my grip on the holster and finished cuffing him.

There he lay on the mezzanine cuffed and cursing and there I was, breathing harder than I had ever done in my life. As I leaned against the booth wondering what the hell happened here, I heard the footsteps of the responding officers.

The sound of the officers rushing to my aid was the best thing I had ever heard. It was over and I had won. I had to win if I wanted to go home safely, that was the only way it could have ended. The man wasn't injured neither was I, so back to the command we went for me to do my paperwork.

After placing the man in the cell, I sat back in my chair and asked him why he did it? Why he had not paid his fare when he knew I was watching him? Why had he fought with me over the price of a lousy token? His answer was profound. "Because I wanted to, that's why," was all he said.

As I sat there completing the paperwork I kept thinking to myself, this guy fought with me because he wanted to. He just wanted to fight. With him reaching for my gun the way he did, this could have been more than just a fight. Someone could have been killed just because he wanted to fight. The paperwork was finished and he was sent off to Central Booking. On his way to jail for what I hoped would be a long time.

Over the next couple of months I waited to be called in for his trial but I never was and I wondered why. The answer to my wondering came in the form of a letter from the Queens District Attorney's office.

Reading the letter I found out the man had been sentenced to time served then released. This meant that the only time he spent in jail was the time it took me to prepare his paperwork and for him to be called to court. No more than three days. With all the charges I had filed on him, the only one that stuck was the fare beating charge. To which he pleaded guilty. The rest were thrown out.

I fought with this guy to save my life and to keep from taking his. He attempted to assault a uniformed police officer and got away with it. This sucked and also sent out a bad message. You could fight with a cop all you wanted as long as he's not injured badly, nothing would be done to you.

This wasn't justice this was bull. Did the judges and lawyers care more for the criminals then they did the cops? Did they feel it was alright for someone to fight with a cop as long as they didn't severely injure the cop? Is this how they felt? If it was, then something was wrong and the cops were fighting a losing battle.

Not long after jumping to this conclusion, I heard an interesting story about another officer that just made me furious. He arrested a male for shooting and robbing someone. While making the arrest, the officer shot the robber who was attempting to flee the crime scene. While fleeing, the robber shot at the officer, forcing the officer to fire his gun to defend himself.

I learned that the attempted murder charge against the robber was thrown out. At his trial he said he was not aiming to kill the officer, he was scared and was only trying to get away, not shoot the officer. Agreeing with the robber, the Judge hearing the case allowed the charges to be dropped.

I remember the Judge said something like he will allow the attempted murder charges to be thrown out because the defendant showed he had no wish to shoot the officer. He was just trying to escape and fired on the officer out of fear. Police officers should realize that when they took the position as an officer, they would some day be shot at and or killed in the line of duty. It's part of their job and they should know that.

The charge of attempted murder against the robber for shooting his victim stuck, he was found guilty and placed in prison. What did that Judge mean? Did he mean that a cop's life isn't worth the same as regular citizens life. Is this what he meant?

Did he also feel that if a firefighter is burned to death in an arson fire that he, or she should have expected to die that way when he or she took the job? Should the person responsible for setting the fire not be charged with his or her death, because the arsonist just wanted to see the building burn and had not intended to kill anyone.

Is this what the Judge meant? What if someone he had sentenced to prison got out and came looking for him? What if that person found him and just wanted to assault the Judge but while doing so ended up killing the Judge.

Should his attacker be charged only with the assault not the murder, because he had not intended to kill the Judge just assault him. In taking the position as Judge he should have expected that one day someone he had sent to prison would seek revenge on him. It's part of his job, isn't it?

I don't know who the Judge was that made those remarks but I do hope that he is no longer on the bench because for the sake of justice we all can do without him.

The man I fought with that faithful day at Court Square was shot and killed sometime later by another officer. He started a fight with the officer and had removed the officer's gun during the fight. Holding onto his service gun, now under the man's control, the officer was able to reach his backup gun and fired, killing the man.

According to me this should have never happened. That man should have been in prison at the time he was shot. He should have been in prison for the fight he had with me. Maybe by going to prison he would have learned that one could not fight a cop and get off totally free. Maybe he would still be alive today...maybe.

I visualize the letter from the District Attorney's office along with my thoughts of the Judge's ruling and I think is it worth it? Is what we as police officers do worth losing our lives over, for some ungrateful people that can't or won't appreciate it. I visualize those papers and wonder still...is it worth it?

▼

CHAPTER 44

SCHOOL DAZE

Thinking back over the years remembering the different adventures that came my way, some were good others were bad. The bad ones stayed with me the longest but the good ones also made an everlasting impression on me.

Take the day that I came across two young students from Newtown High School. I was assigned to cover the school condition for the Grand Ave. station. This is a deceiving station just from looking at it. The station seemed to be small but it's far from small.

There are four exits on the station, two on each of the opposite ends. Located on the different ends of the station there are four high wheel turnstiles. With the four high wheels, passengers that are exiting or entering the station need not pass by the token booth where their movements would be visible to the clerk.

The mezzanine runs the length of Grand Ave. and it's very long and very dark. This is one of those stations that the Transit Authority did not get around to bringing into the new era. The revenue collecting devices are the only upgrades that have been installed. There seems to be little rush to add such things as better lighting, which is a major part of passenger safety.

With the different angles and niches on the station, walking the mezzanine can be a frightening experience. Out of the darkness at any moment could jump a person's worst nightmare. Being as dark as the mezzanine is there would be no warning. Working the station I knew this, I knew where the problem areas were located.

On the back exit there is the stairway that leads to the Queens Blvd exit, which is the closest to the last few stores of the Queens Center mall. With so many stores, the mall is always doing a booming business. The foot traffic is heavy with people looking for bargains or just window-shopping.

Even though this is the closest exit to the stores, I would tell anyone who asked for directions to use the exit on the other end. To me, they would be safer going out that way. That exit was also dark but at least the clerk could see the people. Most of the time when there was an officer assigned to the station, this is where he could be found.

By using this exit, people going to the mall area would only be a half block out of their way but that half block made a big difference in safety. The passengers didn't know this but I did. I tried my best to keep as many people I could from using the back exit.

Along with the shoppers, the school kids also favored the back exit. With the use of the high wheel turnstiles, the school kids could squeeze two or four at a time into the wheel while paying only one fare.

Everyone likes to save money and the kids were big savers. With each fare not paid that gave them more money for the things they wanted, food, video games, whatever they felt the need for.

Saving a fare on the subway won't make you rich, but it will keep change in your pocket. For kids having change is like hitting lotto. When the school let out, flocks of students would gather on the rear of the station. Most of the students were alright, they were just hanging out while waiting for friends to come. Then there were the others. The ones that knew about the students gathering and wanted to prey on them for whatever valuables they carried.

Making several trips to the back exit, I would advise the students to get moving, not to hang around. To them I was the bad guy. Someone else in authority bossing them around telling them what they could and could not do.

While calling me all sorts of names the group would disperse. I didn't care about the name calling as long as they left. They didn't realize I was doing this for their safety, not to be a ball buster. However they looked at what I did, didn't matter as long as they got home safely.

Keeping a crime-free station was my goal. By moving them along I was doing that. Most kids feel that they are immune to bad things happening to them. They will take all sorts of chances but not on my station, I wasn't having it. With me keeping the exits clear and forcing the kids to move along the station was quiet and my day was going well.

Taking a walk to the trouble area, I came across two students I had spoken to earlier. Again, I told them they had to leave. I watched as the pair walked up the stairs to the street.

Returning to the booth area I took up a spot next to the turnstiles and settled in to complete the school condition. As I leaned on the turnstile I heard a large commotion coming from the back area of the station. Turning my head I noticed the same two students I just talk to running towards me.

One of them had blood covering his face. The other was clutching his stomach. Upon reaching me the pair began telling me they were robbed and beaten by two guys that were on the back of the station. They told me after I ran them off the station they waited a few minutes and then returned.

While they hung out, the two robbers came up to them and asked, "You seen any cops?' After telling the robbers that I had gone to the other end of the station the students also told them I was a pain in the ass and would probably be coming back soon.

Agreeing with the students that cops were a pain, the robbers then asked the students for a cigarette. The pair stood around smoking and talking for a minute or two before the robbers asked, "Where do you live, do you guys go to Newtown, you got any friends coming down here?"

Not thinking, the students gave the robbers the answers they were looking for. They didn't live in the area, they did go to Newtown High School and no they did not have any friends coming to the station.

With their next question the robbers set the tone for what was to come. "You got any money, you know what this is, give it up!" Before they could run, the robbers grabbed the students and began beating on them. Raining blows on the students the robbers beat them into submission.

After removing the property they wanted from the students, the robbers warned them not to say anything because if they did, they would find the two and kill them. Happy with their take they fled to the street, while the students ran to find me.

Over the radio I put out a description of the robbers and requested medical assistance for the students. While waiting for the ambulance to arrive, the students told me they were sorry for causing me so many problems and should have listened when I told them to go home.

They told me they had seen me on the station before and liked the way I handled the kids. The reason they were hanging around was because I made them feel safe.

I asked them why they didn't tell me this before because I had no problem with them asking me questions or waiting with me on the station. Kids will be kids and their answer showed this. The young man who was bleeding from his head said, "We can't let others know we like cops, they'll make fun of us, cause nobody is suppose to like cops, you know what I mean?"

Yeah, I did, these were two good kids who had to hide what they felt so they could fit in with their peers. That's the life of a kid, fitting in with others. If you don't fit in, life can be miserable.

With the ambulance taking what seemed to be forever to reach the station, I tied my bandana around the head of the bleeding student. His buddy was lying at my feet still clutching his stomach while crying out in pain. Doing what I could for the young man at my feet, I told Central to put a rush on the ambulance.

Over the radio I heard there were officers searching for the robbers and the ambulance was about three minutes away from reaching the station. I couldn't leave the two wounded students to join in the search, I didn't want to. I had to keep them calm and alert. I didn't know how badly they were hurt and had to be with them if they got worse.

Watching the two in so much pain was hard but there wasn't anything I could do to stop their pain. Trying my best to reassure the pair, I kept telling them we were going to catch the guys that did this to them. Knowing deep down inside that the longer the search went on without any results the harder it was going to be to catch the robbers. Through all their pain, the two students kept on apologizing for the trouble they caused.

As the pair suffered through the pain, other passengers gathered to watch. Looking up at the crowd that gathered the student with the head wound waved for me to come closer to him. Leaning closer to the young man I listened as he told me the two that robbed and beat them was in the crowd. "Are you sure?" I asked. "Yeah that's them," he said, "Over next to the phone, that's them."

Telling the student not to stare at the robbers, to act as if he didn't see them, I stood up straight. In a loud voice making sure the crowd could hear me I said, "I got to make a call, stay here don't move," while winking at the student.

Making my way over to the phone, I could see the two robbers flanking it on each side. Getting my plan of action together I came up with an attack plan. Turning back to look at the fallen students, I removed my mace from my gun belt and held it in my left hand. I was going to mace the robber on the left side of the phone, then pounce on the other.

About two feet away from the phone I said to the unsuspecting robbers, "Excuse me I need the phone." As they started to move aside, I raised my hand

and let go with my mace. A direct hit, I caught the robber on my left with the mace right in his eyes. As he reached for his face while screaming out in pain I jumped on the other.

Before he knew what hit him I had the second robber down on the ground and cuffed. Turning my attention back to his buddy who was now kneeling still covering his burning face, I whipped out my other cuffs and placed them on him.

Both students identified the pair as being the two who robbed and assaulted them. With that the robbers were taken away to jail. The students recovered from their injuries and went on with their lives.

Over the next two years I would run into the pair every once in a while. Whenever we met we would talk and joke. The experience of the robbery had not made them turn away from people. In fact just the opposite, they would assist any person they felt might be in need. The two no longer hid the way they felt about cops.

Another two years had gone by, I had not seen the two young men for some time. I wondered what happened to them and hoped they were alright. I knew if they kept on going about life the way they had the last time I saw them, they would be just fine. If they did that then I didn't have to worry about them.

One day while awaiting roll call I heard this familiar voice say, "Hey old-timer looks like we're with you today." Lifting my head to see who was talking, I found myself looking at the two young men from Grand Ave. that had been so savagely beaten.

It took a moment for me to comprehend what I was seeing but it was true. In front of me stood two new officers beaming with pride. They looked good in their shinny new uniforms, I was very happy to see them.

I stood up from my chair and we embraced each other. For the next three months the young officers were assigned to me for training. They made a request to work with me, which was granted by the Captain after hearing their reasons why. The time I spent with the young officers was great, we learned a great deal about each other and came to be close friends.

The new officers filled me with pride as they told me the reason they became officers was the way I treated them and the way I went about my job. They saw that a cop wasn't someone to be afraid of but someone that was there to help, someone who cared and something that they wanted to be.

Each time I saw the officers over the years I would think back to what they told me and I would say to myself, "Yeah, it's worth it. Doing this job is worth it, there's my proof."

The vision of the two new officers standing in front of me in their shinny new uniforms is a wonderful vision to have and I'll keep it always.

CHAPTER 45

▼

REASONING

Being a cop is the last thing I saw myself as while growing up in Bedford-Stuyvesant, Brooklyn. The cops were looked upon as the enemy and anyone that wanted to be one was labeled the same. The cops weren't the good guys. They were the ones that you ran from. They were the ones that came and took your family or friends away.

The cops were the ones that would shoot you or beat you up for no reason. They could not be trusted and no one wanted to. Being a cop was the last thing I thought I would become, least of all a Transit cop.

What was a Transit cop? I had never heard of such a thing, I didn't even know they existed. The only cops I knew about were the ones I saw on television or the Street cops that I had been brought up to fear and distrust.

Well, I found out what a Transit cop truly is. They are just ordinary people that laugh, bleed, cry and die just like everyone else. Most are not looking for glory or praise. No, the average Transit cop is someone who cares and wants to help. No one ever sees a movie or television show about Transit cops. There aren't any books written about Transit cops, all of these things are reserved for the precinct cops.

Transit cops do the job the Street cops can't or won't. Transit cops are a special breed of officers. They can handle conditions the average Street cop cannot even imagine. Working alone most of their careers, Transit cops must learn to use their minds and bodies to a higher degree than Street cops.

Help isn't around the corner. No, it could be several stations away and take some time in arriving and you pray that the radio works. So when the time comes to handle a situation, a Transit cop had better be ready and able to deal with whatever is thrown at him or her.

Preparing one to become a Transit cop starts from day one of the academy. Now I know why the instructors had us say that cadence over and over again, "WE ARE THE TRANSIT POLICE, THE FEW THE PROUD THE BEST!"

They made us say it because they knew it was true. To the recruits it was a joke but to the instructors they knew it was true. I would come to realize that it is true. "WE ARE THE FEW, WE ARE THE PROUD, AND WE ARE THE BEST!"

I have nothing against the Street cops, what they do is fine. How they do what they do is up to them and I won't question their ways. The only thing I do know for sure is something I was told a long time ago and it has never been proven to be false. An old-timer who I met when I first became a Transit cop related this to me. He said to me:

"Kid, people are going to make fun of you for being a Transit cop. They are going to laugh at you and they aren't going to give you the respect you are entitled. You're gonna get it from the public because they don't know any better. Worst of all you're gonna get it from the Street cops because they wish they could do the job that we do. It takes a special person to make it as a Transit cop and none of the Street cops would be able to cut it. They get all the glory and respect while we don't even get a second thought. Just remember when one of them puts you down for being a Transit cop, it only takes one Transit cop to do what it would take four Street cops, a Sergeant plus a Lieutenant to handle. They wish they could do the job we do day in and day out without recognition. But they can't. So for them to save face they have to try and put us down. As long as they get all the headlines and the praise they will treat us like they do. Just remember we know their biggest secret. They wish they could do what we do, they really want to be like us but they can't. They are too busy chasing the headlines and feeling superior. Ask one of them what they scored on the test they took to become a cop. After they tell you their score tell them yours, smile and say, "So that's how you got stuck in a precinct, I feel sorry for you," then walk away. They know who's the best. They also know that it will never change. Be proud of what you do. Know the only reason they disrespect you is because they're jealous they can't be like you."

What he had told me rang true for many years. Then came the mid ninety's.

CHAPTER 46

▼

ONE BIG HAPPY...

With the Transit police now getting more and more recognition by the city and other states for lowering the number of crimes, we were now the ones grabbing all the headlines.

The lowly Transit police of New York were ranked higher than the glorified Street cops when it came to lowering crime. That could not be, there wasn't any way the Transit police could out-do the Street cops. It had to be stopped.

The only way the city could take credit for our hard work was to take us over. To join forces with us, then claim credit for everything we had done. For them to do this they would say we were going to join them. They were the bigger department so to save us from extinction they would do us a favor by letting us join them.

Along came the merge, a day that will live in infamy. Every piece of superior equipment the Transit police had was taken out of the commands and given to the precincts. All our strategies on dealing with crime were taken, renamed and claimed by the street. They robbed us blind.

The goal of the higher-ups within the Street cops was to tear us apart. They opened up opportunities for officers to transfer between Street and Transit. I think they were hoping that all the Transit cops would run to leave the subways, proving to them how bad it was to work there.

How wrong they were. Not only did the Transit cops not pour out of the subways into the streets, just the opposite was occurring. The Street cops wanted to be Transit cops. Now with the so-called merge they could become Transit cops without being ridiculed. They could now forget the rest and join the best and they did.

They came in droves and they all said the one thing the real Transit cops knew all along. Being a Transit cop was the best-kept secret in the city. After all the years of not giving Transit cops their due, the Street cops were now seeing what I already knew. The grass can be greener on the other side and believe me on our side it was much greener.

The Street cops looked to make us over in their image. We wore their patches and logos. We also took their training, which somehow seemed oddly familiar. They tried their best to make us conform. With all their efforts to erase our memories they were just proving more and more who the best really were.

With the takeover completed they were in charge of the Transit police. We were all one now. No longer were we the Transit Police Department of New York City. We were now known as the New York City Police Department, Transit Division.

They could change our name, but they couldn't change us. We knew who we were and who we would always be. The Transit Police Department of New York City, "THE FEW, THE PROUD, THE BEST!"

Being a Transit cop led me to the visions I have shared with you. Having seen these visions I have come to love life even more. These visions have led to me becoming a stronger person and hopefully a better human being.

As we go through our lives there are many sights we will see and remember from our travels, but the subways of New York City are the only place that can offer the, "Tunnel Visions."

The Subway

Ain't nobody doing it, people need to do it,
That's pay your fare!
Pay my fare?
That's right! Pay your fare!!
Pay my fare? I ain't got no money to ride the subway.
Can you give me some money, to ride the subway?
I really need some money, to ride the subway.
The cost is too high, trains, too slow, you can't smoke your
Cigarette or play your radio, on the subway,

That's the law now! On the subway.
I clock the wheel back, I slide on through,
Then I run and run from the man in blue, in the subway.
He won't catch me!
I walk through the gate when the steel wheels roar,
That's a dollar fifty more I got for the store!
Not the subway!
I'm on the train now, I'm going home now.
Officer can I talk to you?
Yeah what?
I ain't got no money,
My wife's in the hospital,
My dog died,
I ain't eaten in three days,
I'm just trying to get downtown to pick up my check,
I got's ID, give me the summons!
Just give me the summons!
Wait a minute!
You can't lock me up!
Not on the subway!
By W.K. Brown

THE END

978-0-595-35050-6
0-595-35050-X